The Ballad of Crookback & Shakespeare

Clive Greenwood & Jason Wing

TSL Drama

DRAMATIS PERSONAE

WILLIAM SHAKESPEARE

SIR EDMUND TILNEY

(other roles can be doubled and are not gender specific)

QUEEN ELIZABETH I

PHILIP HENSLOWE

ROBERT GREENE

EM BALL

BEN JONSON

TAVERN KEEPER

MISTRESS MONTJOY

MARLOWE

ANNE HATHAWAY

THOMAS KYD

INSTRUMENT (a Hired Thug)

RICHARD TOPCLIFFE

KING JAMES I

JESTER

"VICTORY"

"PEACE"

RICHARD BURBAGE

LAURENCE FLETCHER

HOST

MARION HACKETT

LADY OF THE LAKE

KEILWORTH MEIAL

OFFSTAGE VOICES

Running time

Approx 2 hours

for Michael Leader

1938 – 2016

ACT 1 – 1594

In half-light the cast enter and stand as unrecognizable figures.

They sing   "Lord save our gracious sovereign
Elizabeth by name
That long unto our comfort
She may both rule and reign"

LIGHTS UP on QUEEN ELIZABETH I

QUEEN ELIZABETH: Amongst our guests who will attend us here at Hampton Court is the ambassador of the French King, we wish him to hear a play. We were greatly taken by the fat knight, Falstaff in love, and we wish another play from its writer, we would have a history play showing how our beloved grandfather rescued the realm from the clutches of the usurping Duke of Gloucester. Call forth the Master of the Revels.

          [ELIZABETH imperiously claps her hands, at once figures dart off looking for the errant Sir Edmund Tilney and calling for him]

VOICE 1:   Call forth the Master of the Revels …

VOICE 2:   The Master of the Revels …

VOICE 3:   Sir Edmund Tilney …

VOICE 4:   *[a harlot's voice]* Edmund love, I think they want you.

          [SIR EDMUND TILNEY rushes into the spotlight adjusting his breeches]

ELIZABETH: What kept you Sir Edmund?

TILNEY: Forgive me Your Majesty, I was about the business of the Revels, seeing a supplier of er … stuff.

QUEEN ELIZABETH:	Well, you have new Revels business to attend to. The French Ambassador will shortly visit us at Hampton Court, and we would have ...
TILNEY:	A bear baiting Your Majesty?
ELIZABETH:	May I remind you, the French Ambassador has already seen bear baiting, bull baiting and the ape on horseback, now we will hear a play, a tragedy ...
TILNEY:	A tragedy Your Majesty? Of course. May I be so bold as to suggest the great university wit, Robert Greene?
ELIZABETH:	No, you may not. And he is dead is he not? Do you plan to ask my Conjuror, Dr Dee, to communicate with him in the realm of the dead to demand a play from him? I had no idea the Office of the Revels had such great a reach!
TILNEY:	Your Majesty is correct as always, but the late Robert Greene left behind a large number of writings ...
ELIZABETH:	And a large number of debts also I am told? Mainly with the alehouse. We heard this from the writer whom we commanded to show us Falstaff in love, we were greatly taken with him. What is his name?
TILNEY:	William Shakespeare, Your Majesty. But he has not a university education and therefore he cannot write a tragedy.
ELIZABETH:	We do not care. He is a writer is he not? Therefore, this Master Shakespeare will write us a tragedy.
TILNEY:	Of course, Your Majesty, and may I humbly suggest the classical Greek tragedy of "Orpheus".
ELIZABETH:	Boring! Our negotiations with France are not proceeding well, we feel they need a history

lesson, they need to know with whom they deal when they negotiate with the House of Tudor. Therefore, we will show the French Ambassador how our beloved grandfather King Henry VII rightfully took the crown from the claw-like clutches of that crookbacked child murdering usurping ...

TILNEY: King Richard the Third.

QUEEN ELIZABETH: I think you meant to say, the hated hunchback usurper the Duke of Gloucester.

TILNEY: A slip of the tongue Your Majesty.

QUEEN ELIZABETH: Perhaps it is you who needs the history lesson? Sometimes I wonder why I gave you this position.

[*pause, an awkward silence*]

You are still here Sir Edmund? You may leave The Presence.

TILNEY: Thank you, Your Majesty.

[TILNEY *bows as he backs out*]

BLACKOUT

LIGHTS UP

A portrait of Queen Elizabeth is hanging in the office in the former priory of St John in Clerkenwell created for THE MASTER OF THE REVELS, SIR EDMUND TILNEY. Playscripts are neatly piled upon shelves, with ledgers in neat rows.

ENTER SHAKESPEARE. He looks about, he sees the wine jug and smells it approvingly, he thinks to pour himself a goblet, then thinks again, he goes to the portrait of the Queen and toasts her with an empty goblet which he then puts down.

SIR EDMUND TILNEY enters from an unseen door.

SHAKESPEARE walks to the fireplace and warms himself.

TILNEY:	The weather is somewhat chill now, is it not Master Shakespeare? Yes, I fear autumn is now upon us, that is the first time I have ordered a servant to lay a fire to counteract the "chilling Autumn".
	[SHAKESPEARE *is scribbling this down using an inkhorn around his neck*]
TILNEY:	You are welcome to warm yourself with some wine, and thank you for showing some restraint, unlike some I could mention, Ben Jonson, Thomas Nashe, sots and malt worms both.
	[TILNEY *pours* SHAKESPEARE *a wine*]
TILNEY:	Better than you get in "The Mermaid" I warrant? Master Shakespeare, the point of this meeting is that Her Majesty was greatly taken by your play performed at Windsor this summer with … oh what is his name? The fat drunkard?
SHAKESPEARE:	Richard Burbage? Oh no that was the actor who played him! The character is Falstaff, Sir John Falstaff.

TILNEY:	Ah yes Falstaff, a rehashing of your cowardly knight Fastolfe from "Harry Sixth"?
SHAKESPEARE:	Sir Edmund, I am honoured you know my work.
TILNEY:	Do not flatter yourself Master Shakespeare, I am not one of the beardless boys who argue incessantly who is their playhouse favourite. I am the Master of the Revels and it is my duty to know everything that goes on –
	[TILNEY *indicates his meticulously neat and orderly desk*]
	And everything I allow to go on at the Playhouses.
	[TILNEY *indicates the playscripts piled upon shelves*]
SHAKESPEARE:	So many plays!
TILNEY:	All registered, read and licensed, if I see fit. I pride myself Master Shakespeare that I keep a well-ordered office. Let us put it to the test, when did you first come to my attention? No do not tell me.
	[TILNEY *goes to the ledgers, removes and reads one*]
	Here we are – William Shakespeare, "Harry the Sixth" 1592 for Philip Henslowe, remarkable.
SHAKESPEARE:	You are too kind Sir Edmund.
TILNEY:	What? No! Not the play, it went on a bit, that's what I heard, I meant you, the man of mystery, nothing on you, and then suddenly there you are at the Rose.
SHAKESPEARE:	The Rose, yes of course, I had not long been in London then …

Flashback scene The Rose

SHAKESPEARE *enters with* PHILIP HENSLOWE.

HENSLOWE: Well done Will.

SHAKESPEARE: You are pleased Master Henslowe?

HENSLOWE: Away with you with this "Master Henslowe"! I am "Philip" to my boys! Of course, I am pleased, another full house for Harry the Sixth, a fine jingling purse to be entered up in my diary. You've a knack for this writing Will, and not many actors have I tell you that. Not that I know much about it, I'm a businessman, a dyer, that was my trade, even now I can name you any colour someone is wearing.

[HENSLOWE *points at people in the audience*]

HENSLOWE: Lady Blush, Lusty Gallant, Sick Spaniard, and Puke! Come on Will, I will stand you a drink.

SHAKESPEARE: That is kind of you but …

HENSLOWE: But? But what? Listen all the lads here will tell you, if the governor stands you a drink you don't say no. We don't see you in the alehouse after the play, which concerns me.

SHAKESPEARE: It is just …

HENSLOWE: It concerns me because I didn't build an alehouse next to the Rose, because it looks nice, it's part of the business. It's where we work them into the net so to speak. Oh God that's all we need.

SHAKESPEARE: What?

HENSLOWE: Robert bloody Greene.

SHAKESPEARE: Greene? Greene was here today?

HENSLOWE: Yes. That's him over there in the goose turd green cloak, how appropriate! No doubt coming to see what all the fuss is about, the new writer that all London is talking of.

SHAKESPEARE: I have read everything Greene has written, "Friar Bacon & Friar Bungay", "Orlando Furioso", his books about London crime, although my wife would not approve of them.

HENSLOWE: Your wife? I did not know you to be wed Will.

SHAKESPEARE: Yes, and we have children to bless us.

HENSLOWE: Is that why you don't join us?

[SHAKESPEARE *nods*]

HENSLOWE: I understand. You will make a good husband and father, not like that arsehole Greene, left his wife and son, for that trollop Em Ball, her husband not long done the Tyburn jig and she takes up with Greene.

[ROBERT GREENE *accompanied by his flashy mistress* EM BALL *interrupts*]

GREENE: Henslowe!

HENSLOWE: Master Greene. You are welcome.

SHAKESPEARE: Sir it is an honour to meet you.

GREENE: The honour is all yours I assure you.

[GREENE *snaps his fingers imperiously*]

A bottle of your finest Rhenish wine, I have my own tankard, and two goblets.

[GREENE *hands one goblet to* EM BALL *and another to* HENSLOWE *pointedly ignoring* SHAKESPEARE — *there is an awkward pause*]

SHAKESPEARE: What are you working on at the moment Master Greene?

GREENE: Trying to drink in peace, without being asked stupid questions.

EM BALL: Robert, go easy on him, he's only a lad.

GREENE: "A looking glass for London".

SHAKESPEARE:	Yes indeed! that's what the playhouse should be, where ordinary people can see themselves ...
GREENE:	What? I wasn't talking to you. That is the play we agreed did we not Henslowe? Em!

[*he snaps his fingers.* EM BALL *hands over a manuscript*]

HENSLOWE:	That's right.
GREENE:	Now I must put money in my purse, so I will request my fee.

[HENSLOWE *brings out some coins, they are clearly not enough, and* GREENE *indicates with fingers he wants more*]

You have a great writer of books, deigning to write for the playhouse, and that costs.

HENSLOWE:	If I may give you some advice, from Edward Alleyn.
GREENE:	I am Robert Greene, and I do not take advice from anyone, least of all actors.
HENSLOWE:	Well, I am Philip Henslowe, owner of the Rose Theatre, and Alleyn is my leading actor.
GREENE:	And your son in law.
HENSLOWE:	That matters not. He said your last play was too long, too slow, and not enough action, people left before the end.
GREENE:	It's not my fault if my words and ideas are too rich for the Rose's rabble to understand.
HENSLOWE:	No one left today, we were turning them away.

[HENSLOWE *indicates* SHAKESPEARE]

The lad is popular Robert.

GREENE:	Is he indeed? And it's "Master Greene" to you.

[GREENE *makes his way over to* SHAKESPEARE *who is being "talked at" by* EM BALL]

EM BALL:	Yeah, my old man used to do most things, you know, highway robbery, cutpurse, bit of murder, you know how it is, but then he got into being a "prigger of prancers".
	[SHAKESPEARE *looks blank*]
EM BALL:	A horse thief! Till he nicked one belonging to Richard Topcliffe, you know, the torturer? Has his own torture chamber in his house apparently. Well, more people are working from home now aren't they, since the plague?
GREENE:	So Master Shakescene ...
SHAKESPEARE:	Shakespeare Sir, William Shakespeare.
GREENE:	So Shaxper, you set yourself quite a task, Henry the Sixth could be considered a dull king ...
SHAKESPEARE:	Indeed Sir, but I think the very fact of his being a cipher, a blank canvas if you will, makes it more interesting to have great characters around him ...
GREENE:	And a dull king could make a dull play, which it did. I understand Henry remained silent for years, please emulate him and do not write again.
SHAKESPEARE:	Sir with respect, a writer must learn his craft ...
GREENE:	Not at the expense of the paying public.
HENSLOWE:	The house was full Rob ... Master Greene.
EM BALL:	He's right you know Robert, packed it was!
SHAKESPEARE:	And yes, it needs work, I know, but some of the characters worked I feel, take Richard, Duke of Gloucester.
EM BALL:	Oh yes, he was good, the crookback.
GREENE:	Of course, you brought in the future Richard the Third — you had him kill the Duke of Somerset, and Clifford too? Unbelievable.

SHAKESPEARE:	Really?
TILNEY:	Yes. Totally unbelievable, the real Richard the Third would have been two at the time, if we had two-year-olds who could kill like that, a nursery nurse and a couple of her charges could have wiped out the Armada before they had learned to wipe their arses.
SHAKESPEARE:	I was not writing history but dramatizing it.
GREENE:	No. You simply rehashed a dull play about a dull king who lost us Anjou and Maine. That's all you have – bombast.
EM BALL:	Sorry, he gets like this when he's been drinking, I wish he wouldn't.

[for the first time we see a softer, more worried side of EM]

GREENE:	That is all you are capable of, bombasting, padding out old plays with your execrable blank verse. What will you rehash next I wonder? "The Troublesome Reign of King John" perhaps? It's about time that crawled out again, or "The Famous Victories of Henry V" – well what is it to be?
SHAKESPEARE:	Titus Andronicus.
GREENE:	Never heard of it.
SHAKESPEARE:	No, you wouldn't. I haven't written it yet. I have so many stories here in my head, they demand to be told, I see them, a magical wood, enchantment, fairies ...
EM BALL:	Oh, that sounds nice, when is that going to be on?
SHAKESPEARE:	Then one about an old drunkard, fooling himself he is still young, consorting with harlots.

[this is getting a bit near the mark for GREENE *and* EM BALL!]

	But he never realises his time is over. Then a magical island.
GREENE:	Where?
SHAKESPEARE:	In my mind.
GREENE:	Where do you see this island? Come on Shakescene, with your original ideas, where is it?
SHAKESPEARE:	Er ... off the coast of ... Bohemia.
GREENE:	You idiot! Bohemia is a landlocked country! It's in the middle of Europe. It doesn't have a coast.
SHAKESPEARE:	I admit my geography can be a bit hazy, but I am more concerned with the characters, the story and the plot of the play, "the play's the thing". Unlike the University Wits I do not need to peer at maps to entertain the common man.

[GREENE *suddenly menaces* SHAKESPEARE]

GREENE:	Listen! You might think because you have given Henslowe a success with this putrid pageant you penned, and saved him money because you acted in it too, badly I might add, I hate actors, superfluous sort of men, you now think you are the Johannes Factotum of the Playhouse, but I tell you what you are, it begins with "C", no not that – but you definitely are one of those. You are an Upstart Crow, beautified with OUR feathers. You know why I am such a success with my books of London crime? Because the cozeners, coney catchers and cutthroats are my people now, I have thrown in my lot with them for better or worse. I could have your throat cut in a dark alley, so stay away from me, if you know what's good for you, got that country boy? Come Em, Henslowe will settle up for the worst Rheinish I have ever tasted.

[GREENE *strides out to leave with* EM b*ehind, she turns*]

EM BALL:	Sorry, he gets a bit funny when he's had a few … maybe we'll come and see your play about the fairies.
GREENE:	Em!
EM BALL:	Sorry got to go. I liked the Crookback, by the way, scary, but a bit, well seductive, you know? That bit when he wants the crown for himself "like a far off shore where he would tread".
	[SHAKESPEARE *applauds* EM's *reading of the line, she is pleased.* GREENE *turns, impatient to leave*]
GREENE:	Perhaps it's the shore of Bohemia.
	[GREENE *roughly bundles her out. They both EXIT*]
HENSLOWE:	You alright Will?
	[SHAKESPEARE *nods*]
	They say, don't they, never meet your idols? And don't put them on a pedestal – when they fall off, they can hurt you.
BLACKOUT	

LIGHTS UP

Back in the Revels Office.

SHAKESPEARE: Greene had a fine mind till drink took it, and he drank enough of that Rheinish wine to float the Queen's new battleship.

TILNEY: Could not you leave him with a little dignity, to be remembered well?

SHAKESPEARE: Oh, he will be, his comments about the "Upstart Crow" will I wager ne'er be forgot, well for as long as I live at least.

TILNEY: We'll see. Now, back to business. Her Majesty requires a tragedy about Richard Duke of Gloucester.

SHAKESPEARE: Richard the Third?

TILNEY: Or as the Queen would have it "the child murdering usurper", and we have a problem.

SHAKESPEARE: Indeed, King Richard has so many sides to him.

TILNEY: Just the one with the hump will do. Remind me Master Shakespeare which university did you attend?

SHAKESPEARE: I like to say The University of Life, where …

TILNEY: So, you did not attend a university? Why not just say so for God's sake? But you have now been commissioned to write a Tragedy, a style of play, may I remind you, that has always been the sole prerogative of a university educated man.

SHAKESPEARE: Though I have not been to university and I cannot read the Greeks, I have studied the great Roman writers, and I am more than capable of writing a tragedy for our Queen than you give me credit for.

TILNEY:	This tragedy the Queen requires is about the most notorious tyrant Crookback Richard. Time is pressing. Now you tossed off in a matter of days that ridiculous farce about Falstaff leaving Eastcheap for Windsor, to try to bed a lot of slatternly strumpets, and that amused the Queen. So, this should present no problem for you. In seven days, you will return here, and as is usual read me the play, which if suitable I will licence, register and allow. Do you follow me Master Shakespeare?
SHAKESPEARE:	Er yes, seven days are not much to tell such great history.
TILNEY:	History? Hmm? The Queen's idea of entertaining foreign ambassadors is watching bears, bulls and dogs ripping each other apart, so I wouldn't try anything too arty.

TILNEY dismisses SHAKESPEARE

LIGHTING CHANGE TO A DIMLY LIT TAVERN

SHAKESPEARE is in a tavern with BEN JONSON who has clearly been there a lot longer and imbibed more than he has.

JONSON:	Sit yourself down, Will, that wench won't be interested in you, you're a writer, not a player and a bad one at that!
SHAKESPEARE:	Really? I can write three plays in the time it takes you to dip your quill.
JONSON:	Which you won't be doing with her! And I wrote "Volpone" in a dozen days, while working my way through a Lordly gift of a dozen bottles of sack.
SHAKESPEARE:	A bottle a day? That explains much. Perhaps when I am as successful as you, they will call me "Will the Conqueror".
JONSON:	Well, you won't be conquering any wenches

drinking that womanly wine, I drink well and have brave notions ...

SHAKESPEARE: And often you drink **too** well, and have foolish notions, that you then put in plays that land you in gaol.

JONSON: I can drink more in two hours than a Frenchman can in twenty-four.

SHAKESPEARE: Yes well, I think they see it more as a social event rather than a competition.

JONSON: Wine and water! Ale not good enough for you now Will?

SHAKESPEARE: Well, you know Ben [*exaggerated posh accent*] "when one is at Court one must drink like a gentleman".

JONSON: Since when were you at Court? A courtyard is more our style!

SHAKESPEARE: I was at the Office of the Revels today ...

JONSON: You have my deepest sympathy. I am sure Tilney was his usual welcoming self, showing his great love for playwrights. It's ridiculous, the man's in charge of the playhouses, and never sets foot in one. You know they had him in mind as ambassador to Spain?

SHAKESPEARE: [*incredulous*] No!

JONSON: It's true! Can you imagine? Give him a week there he would have started another war! We would have had a second Armada on the way. Mind you, I thought if he had buggered off to annoy Philip of Spain, I could apply for his job.

SHAKESPEARE: What? The King of Spain? I don't think they advertise the vacancy on a pillar at St Paul's, and I didn't have you down for a ... you know ...

[SHAKESPEARE *jokingly makes the sign of the cross*]

JONSON:	Very funny Will, I meant Tilney's job!
SHAKESPEARE:	YOU! The Master of the Revels! Don't make me laugh Ben! The Bishop of Winchester has got more chance of being Pope than you have of being Master of the Revels, and My Lord Bishop, may I remind you, not being a man who dwells too deeply on the requirements of Holy Office, owns every brothel on Bankside! I have been invited back at Court by a certain lady.
JONSON:	Ooh, a dark lady?
SHAKESPEARE:	Not dark up top.
JONSON:	Oh! Her! She wants more Falstaff from you, does she? Well, she has had Falstaff in love, where will she have him now, [*mimes pulling down his breeches*] on her privy? In her bedchamber?
	[*the* TAVERN KEEPER *looks through the door at them and exits*]
SHAKESPEARE:	Be quiet Ben! That's sedition. The Queen's spies and Tilney's men are everywhere.
JONSON:	You think I fear them? T'were best rip forth their tongues, scar out their eyes when next they come, a fit reward for spies. I have been a soldier and would run them through with my weapon with ease.
	[JONSON *quite drunk draws his sword and starts to brandish it, the* TAVERN KEEPER *looks in suspiciously and withdraws again*]
SHAKESPEARE:	In God's name, put your weapon away Ben. No, it is not more Falstaff she wants. She requires Richard the Third and it is to be delivered in seven days.
JONSON:	Could be interesting, they liked him when you put him Harry Sixth. Mind you, I have got a pretty shrewd suspicion why she wants the

	Crookback. So, my noble courtier, do you have anything to bestow upon a poor soldier and a humble bricklayer and sometime writer like me?
SHAKESPEARE:	Well Burbage is still waiting for "Everyman in his Humour" which you promised us over a year ago.
JONSON:	I am not a hack like you Will, I take time to craft my work, I take inspiration from the classics, true, but not like some sea beast that swallows all, crude, raw and undigested, but rather one that can concoct, divide, and turn all to nourishment, and unlike you I do not pillage from the quills of dead writers.
SHAKESPEARE:	I do not "pillage" Ben but cherish the memory and work of one who was taken too soon.
	[SHAKESPEARE *stands and raises his goblet*]
	To Christopher Marlowe.
	[JONSON *unsteadily toasts back*]
SHAKESPEARE:	So "Everyman in his Humour" is STILL not ready? Nor do I believe ever will be. I take my leave. Ben Jonson, you ever were a slow thing, and when we ask you for a play – why then you give us "no thing". Good night Ben.
	[*as* SHAKESPEARE *goes to leave* BEN JONSON *produces a rolled up manuscript and brandishes it like a sword maybe smacking* SHAKESPEARE *on the backside with it*]
JONSON:	Here my noble courtier Shakespeare, my sword is unsheathed again.
	[SHAKESPEARE *turns horrified, the* TAVERN KEEPER *returns*]
JONSON:	But now my weapon is words.
	[JONSON *mock stabs* SHAKESPEARE *with it.*

	SHAKESPEARE *takes it and starts to read it*]
SHAKESPEARE:	What is this? The "Isle of Dogs"?
JONSON:	Where the blatant Beast doth rule and reign, and all the most notorious villains came, Royalty included.
TAVERN KEEPER:	Any more sedition and you are out!
JONSON:	It's not "sedition" Tapster, it's satire.
TAVERN OWNER:	I don't care what it is, and I am not a tapster, this is my tavern and I know where the Constables reside.
SHAKESPEARE:	There is no need for the Constables, mine host.
	[SHAKESPEARE *gently leads the* TAVERN OWNER *out, reassuring him all the way, before returning to* JONSON]
JONSON:	It's ridiculous. What the hell is going to happen to this country when she goes? You're a father too Will, what kind of country are our children going to grow up in? One where they burn people as part of a show? Not even Henslowe went that far.
SHAKESPEARE:	What are you talking about?
JONSON:	In Spain they call it the *"auto da fe"*.
SHAKESPEARE:	The act of Faith …
JONSON:	Very good! Which consists of burning so called "heretics". It could happen here. That mad Spaniard still thinks he should be King of England.
	[*the* TAVERN OWNER *is back*]
TAVERN OWNER:	I heard that! Treason! You said that a Spaniard should be King!
JONSON:	Is it your usual practice to listen to private conversations? Well you won't, not without your ears!

[JONSON starts *to wave his sword close to the* TAVERN KEEPER]

SHAKESPEARE: Ben! I apologise, he has just had too much of your good strong ale, please we are about to take our leave.

TAVERN KEEPER: See that you do.

[TAVERN KEEPER *leaves*]

SHAKESPEARE: Ben. A thief in a playwright's drunken mouth that steals his brains, will see him dead if he does not have a care. And it's not fair on the taverners, they are ordinary working people, trying to make a living. They are afraid Ben, when you speak like that, it's sedition.

JONSON: No! It's science. Will, we are both men of learning, she is beyond childbearing age, but no one will talk about it, we writers have a duty, to provide the "Staple of News" to tell the people what is going on, not like that ponce Spencer writing her "The Faerie Queen" when he was pretending to be a soldier for her in Ireland, I suspect he didn't try it out on the natives,

[JONSON *puts on a terrible Irish accent*]

"Here you go, sure you'll love this, a sycophantic crawling lickspittle epistle to your Protestant Queen".

SHAKESPEARE: Ben, that is the worst Irish accent I have ever heard! And I recall you wrote her "Cynthia's Revels", or have you forgotten that?

JONSON: That was just for coin, but now I have written her a sequel. My quill is a serpent's tongue, venom is my ink, my paper, this sin-loaded city, there I shall write words sharper than quill of porcupine. I'll dedicate it to the soldiers and sailors that she never paid for the Armada, do you think she'll like it?

[BEN JONSON *picks up the "Isle of Dogs" script and gives an impromptu drunken performance, throughout which he drunkenly dodges the horrified* SHAKESPEARE *who is trying to grab the script from him or shut him up*]

"Good people of Albion, Cynthia's Revels now are ended, the sluttish launderess who made courtiers soil their breeches with excitement will soon be gone. England is now the Isle of Dogs, who will you have as your ruler? The Essex Roaring Boy? The Girl King of Scotland? Satan's Spaniard with his Inquisition? And no one expects them! None are worthy my friends, let us crown Martin the Ape!

[*there is a general melee,* JONSON *ends up confronted by the* TAVERN KEEPER *who enters with a cudgel and threatens* JONSON *with it*]

TAVERN KEEPER:	Get him out of here now, or there will be no need to call the Constables.
SHAKESPEARE:	Silence your mouth Ben or you will get us all hung, drawn and quartered.
JONSON:	Unlike you Will, and her little squirting boys at Court, I feel no need to put my tongue up the Queen's royal passage.

[SHAKESPEARE *grabs the* TAVERN KEEPER's *cudgel and threatens* JONSON]

SHAKESPEARE:	No more about the Queen, Ben, or I will cudgel what little brains you have left myself.
JONSON:	Where is "gentle Shakespeare" now?
SHAKESPEARE:	Gentle Shakespeare wants to provide for his family, like a gentleman, and not get hung like a common traitor.
JONSON:	A gentleman? Well, be a man, put the cudgel down, draw your sword and duel with me.
SHAKESPEARE:	I have no sword, like you have no wit …

JONSON: No wit? You think I cannot write?

SHAKESPEARE: Oh, you can write Ben, but this satire you
                   propose will be the death of us all. So, write it
                   Ben, get the playhouses closed down, see our
                   host here ruined as you get every tavern on
                   Bankside shut down, get the Watermen thrown
                   out of work, see how they will thank you for it,
                   you won't survive a week.

BLACKOUT

BEN JONSON *exits*

LIGHTS UP

SHAKESPEARE *has arrived at his lodgings in Bishopsgate and is having a conversation with his landlady* MISTRESS MONTJOY.

MONTJOY: You're back late Master Shakespeare.

SHAKESPEARE: I met Ben Jonson on Bankside and sometimes an evening with Ben is like listening to someone banging a very large drum in a very small room!

MONTJOY: If you ask me, he is a pestilent fellow.

SHAKESPEARE: But he's the wittiest bricklayer in England, and he is my friend.

MONTJOY: I think he drinks too much.

SHAKESPEARE: True, but when sober he has a fine mind, to his credit.

MONTJOY: He was lodging with her across the way, until she threw him out. And talking of credit, if you could see your way to clearing last week's rent?

SHAKESPEARE: Of course, Mistress Montjoy, as soon as this playscript is delivered I shall receive cash most justly paid.

MONTJOY: And what is your new play to be?

SHAKESPEARE: Well, stall this in your bosom …

MONTJOY: Will Shakespeare! And you a married man!

SHAKESPEARE: Tis a secret that must be locked within the teeth and the lips.

MONTJOY: My lips are sealed.

SHAKESPEARE: Do not tell your gossips, but it is another play for the Queen.

MONTJOY: Oh Will! That's so exciting! Is it the one about the fairies you were telling me about?

SHAKESPEARE: Not quite! It's about Richard the Third.

MONTJOY:	Oh! That's not very jolly.
SHAKESPEARE:	Er … no, I suppose not.
MONTJOY:	Killing those two little boys in the Tower. What does she want a play about him for?
SHAKESPEARE:	It's not proved he killed the princes, but it is not for us to question the Queen.
MONTJOY:	True! She won't be at the beck and call of any man.
OFFSTAGE:	[*a male voice shouts*] Wife
MONTJOY:	Unlike me! Good night to you Will.
	[MONTJOY *exits.* SHAKESPEARE *heads to his desk and sits and starts to write*]
SHAKESPEARE:	Weary from toil, I haste me to my bed, but then begins a journey in my head. Seven days, well here we go. The Princes in the Tower, but how do we know he killed them? Why does the Queen want this?
	[CHRISTOPHER MARLOWE *appears as if in a dream, for the rest of the scene* SHAKESPEARE *sits in chair and is half asleep as things AND PEOPLE come to him*]
MARLOWE:	I can guess why Will, and so can you if you put your mind to it.
	[MARLOWE *stays and haunts the room*]
SHAKESPEARE:	Kit? Kit Marlowe? But you are "the dead shepherd" now.
MARLOWE:	I come to haunt and warn you. Let but a man die and before we are cold in our graves, some damned ditties made, which makes our ghosts walk. Look to the past Will if you want the answer.
	[SHAKESPEARE *glances at a ring he wears and reads the inscription on it*]

SHAKESPEARE:	"Truth betrays not". You gave me this ring Anne when I pledged you my love.
MARLOWE:	Write what may be the truth and maybe it will lose you your head.
	[SHAKESPEARE *picks up a piece of parchment to write on but sees it already has writing on it*]
SHAKESPEARE:	The poem I wrote for you Anne, when first we met.
	[*the 25 year-old* ANNE HATHAWAY *enters the scene.* WILL *in his mind is 18 again*]
SHAKESPEARE:	I've missed you Anne. I have missed your hand on mine.
ANNE:	What other part of me have you missed Will?
SHAKESPEARE:	I have missed all of your parts.
ANNE:	I knew it. You want me for my privy parts. Nothing else.
SHAKESPEARE:	No, Anne. That is not the truth, I have thought about you a lot, enough to write a poem for you.
ANNE:	You foolish boy, I cannot read.
SHAKESPEARE:	I wrote it in my mind for you Anne.
ANNE:	You mean you picked it from a book to recite?
MARLOWE:	Many a lovesick fool recites some flowery nonsense stolen from a book of verse.
SHAKESPEARE:	Some gossips say that I read more than I labour, but I did write something just for you I swear, hear this Anne and you will know I am true in my affection for you.
ANNE:	Let's hear it then, but be warned, I will know if you are lying. Truth betrays not, Will. I'm wiser in my years, as well as older than you.
SHAKESPEARE:	"Shall I compare thee to a summer's day? Thou art more lovely and more temperate, rough

winds do shake the darling buds of May".

MARLOWE: At least I nearly saw May out Will, they took me on its last day in leafy Deptford, close by The Golden Hinde which round the globe has run and matched in race the chariot of the sun. Thou little knowest how in the end thou shalt be visited.

ANNE: Get away with you and your poetry. You're not old enough to wear a codpiece, let alone go courting.

SHAKESPEARE: I am big enough to fill my codpiece though Anne.

MARLOWE: Oh really? I wish you had told me that when I was still alive! Bit late now!

ANNE: Yes, but are you big enough to fill an older woman young Will?

[ANNE and MARLOWE close in on SHAKESPEARE as if both seducing him]

SHAKESPEARE: Are you not intact then?

MARLOWE: Cut to the chase Will, why don't you?

ANNE: I am! What do you take me for? But I am also but flesh and blood and have visited upon myself.

SHAKESPEARE: So you have visited upon yourself in your own bedchamber Anne?

MARLOWE: I think we have established that.

ANNE: Sometimes, but on occasion out in the fields when the sun beat down and I thought no one could see. Do you like that Will?

SHAKESPEARE: Sometimes too hot the eye of Heaven shines.

ANNE: I would not have Heaven's eye upon me, when I visit myself, yours, however, I would not be averse to Will!

MARLOW:	What's it like to be with a woman Will?
SHAKESPEARE:	It fills my loins with fire. There is a kind of passionate wisdom in an older woman that can keep a young man out of the taverns Anne.
ANNE:	I do know such things that would keep you out of the taverns and in my bedchamber Will Shakespeare.
MARLOWE:	It may be a little crowded in there, with that dark girl who haunts the playhouses, not to mention Southampton, remember Will how we used to laugh when we were at the Rose? "He's in again to see the boys, Grisly Wriothesley". [pronounced "Risley"]
SHAKESPEARE:	I would rather be in you than in the taverns Anne.
MARLOWE:	And they say romance is dead! I will stick to tobacco and boys!
ANNE:	Will, are you constant? The sundial grows ever dark for me, I'm not looking for a greyhound out of the slips.
SHAKESPEARE:	I'm looking to make long sport with you Anne.
ANNE:	Longer than a winter's night?
SHAKESPEARE:	Longer than a summer's day.
ANNE:	Longer than a week in the hay?
SHAKESPEARE:	Longer than a month in a farmer's field Anne.
ANNE:	You sound serious Will.
SHAKESPEARE:	How about longer than many years in your embrace Anne?
ANNE:	Do you mean for all time?
MARLOWE:	Time is. Time was. Time will be.
SHAKESPEARE:	As spoke by the Brazen Head of Robert Greene.
ANNE:	What do you mean Will? Is that from one of his ungodly books?

SHAKESPEARE:	The head is magic; it foresees the future. Yes, for eternity Anne. I am ready to settle.
ANNE:	Now it is my turn to ask. Are you intact Will?
SHAKESPEARE:	I have made some sport with the wenches in the field, but only like a foolish boy who struggles with his Latin.
MARLOWE:	He has but small Latin and little Greek ...
ANNE:	So. You are ready for a woman now Will?
MARLOWE:	You can't tell her of your patron can you Will?
SHAKESPEARE:	Yes. I am Anne. For you I am more ready than the greyhound in the slips you spoke of. So, will it Anne if I lie with you.
MARLOWE:	Or **to** you ...
ANNE:	Have you more of that poem you made in your mind for me?
SHAKESPEARE:	Yes. "For as long as men can breathe or eyes can see, so long lives this, and this gives life to thee".
MARLOWE:	Now give her Sonnet 26 "Lord of my Love", who could that be for?
SHAKESPEARE:	I created it in my mind's eye just for you.
ANNE:	You are a clever young boy with your words. You could be a writer Will.
MARLOWE:	He could be the greatest writer of all time, if he can please his Queen, and he needs to get back to "Richard Crookback".
SHAKESPEARE :	I'm a man not a boy Anne, and there is not the money for me to go to university and study, but if I can write all that is in my head, I believe it will please not just you, but the highest in the land, it could bring me enough wealth to buy that.
	[SHAKESPEARE *points*, ANNE *looks*]

ANNE:	New Place? The grandest house in Stratford? Well, you think big Will I give you that! Well best make a start, write more in your mind for me then.
SHAKESPEARE:	I shall Anne Hathaway for as long as I am Will Shakespeare of New Place.
ANNE:	Away with your boasting. And away with you for now Will. We have conversed too long. People will talk.
SHAKESPEARE:	I will away and write your poem down for you Anne lest I forget it. See you at the next nightfall Anne. And I'll have more special words for you, writ with passion.
ANNE:	Keep it in your breeches and keep your loins strong for me. If you prove constant I may in time unsheathe your sword for you.
	[MARLOWE and ANNE exit
	SHAKESPEARE awakes with a start]
SHAKESPEARE:	Anne? Kit?
	[he realizes he is alone. He looks at what he has written]
	"The True Tragedy of Richard of Gloucester, The Princes in the Tower, question mark. Enter Poetry and Truth", is that it? Nothing more?
	[his head slumps on the table. MARLOWE appears]
MARLOWE:	You need more than that Will, if you want those riches "wedges of gold, heaps of pearls" – the Queen likes those, "inestimable stones, unvalued jewels", they lie in "dead men's skulls". You remember Will how we would write and laugh together at my lodgings, me and Kyd, thinking up the most outrageous names for characters to give Tilney an apoplexy? That which fed me destroyed me. Will, remember

me, revenge my foul and most unnatural
MURDER!

[SHAKESPEARE *starts awake. He is alone,*
MARLOWE *has gone, the* WATCHMAN *outside*
shouts]

VOICE OF WATCHMAN: Midnight and all is well, God save the
Queen.

SHAKESPEARE: God save the Queen, and God help me, "call
back yesterday, bid time return!"

LIGHTS DOWN

LIGHTS UP

SHAKESPEARE *and* TILNEY *at the Revels Office.*

TILNEY:	Master Shakespeare – just in the nick of time, the play was due today.
	[TILNEY *picks up and reads*]
SHAKESPEARE:	Forgive me. I have been toiling late to get it right.
TILNEY:	You seem somewhat out of breath, did you put your quill down and run like a greyhound here?
SHAKESPEARE:	Indeed. I lost track of time at my desk.
TILNEY:	I suppose you will be wanting some wine to cool your fevered brow.
	[TILNEY *pours* SHAKESPEARE *some wine*]
SHAKESPEARE:	Thank you Sir Edmund.
TILNEY:	I sometimes think the contents of my cellar is the only reason you writers come to the Office of the Revels.
SHAKESPEARE:	Not at all Sir Edmund, will it please you I read the script of ...
TILNEY:	"The True Tragedy of King Richard the Third".
	[TILNEY *flicks through the pages*]
	I am on the first page Master Shakespeare, but sadly the Crookback is not.
SHAKESPEARE:	I do not believe that is the correct way for the play to open, to show the main protagonist so early.
TILNEY:	Let us see what you have written. "Enter Poetry and Truth", well I don't like either of those.
	[TILNEY *crosses this through with his quill*]
SHAKESPEARE:	[*Sotto voce*] Especially the latter.

TILNEY:	I beg your pardon?
SHAKESPEARE:	Nothing Sir Edmund. There is a ghost.
TILNEY:	Oh yes. The ghost of Lord Stanley.
	[TILNEY *does a ghost noise*]
	Wooh! – I am quaking in my boots, if you are going to do it, do it properly, give the Queen a treat, a gallery of ghosts.
SHAKESPEARE:	I quite liked the ghost.
TILNEY:	No.
SHAKESPEARE:	Maybe I will save that ghost for another play.
	[TILNEY *returns to marking the play*]
TILNEY:	The distresses of Henry the Sixth – just about, the acquisition of the crown by Richard – that needs to be bigger – the landing of Henry Tudor – you need to make him much more heroic, write him a nice speech like Henry the Fifth.
SHAKESPEARE:	"The bloody dog is dead".
TILNEY:	No. It needs to be longer than that. Here you describe the Crookback King as "valiant minded", that will not please our Queen.
SHAKESPEARE:	With respect I believe Her Majesty wants more from her entertainment then just stock characters, as in the old morality play.
TILNEY:	Do you presume to know the Queen's mind?
SHAKESPEARE:	No Sir Edmund, but I know she has a keen mind for plays and is well respected amongst the players. Before each performance we go down on our knees and ask a blessing for the Queen and our patron.
TILNEY:	Yes. I have heard you do much service for your patron on your knees.
SHAKESPEARE:	Sir Edmund, you accused me of "presuming to know the Queen's mind", but I wish only to

	know what my gracious Royal patron wants from me.
TILNEY:	What the Queen always wants, to impress the French King. And what better way to impress him then to show his ambassador the power of the House of Tudor? A play showing them defeating a usurping ruler, being offered the crown by a grateful nation.
SHAKESPEARE:	I have misunderstood Sir Edmund, I thought Her Majesty required a play about the last Plantagenet King, but rather it seems the Queen would instead have a play about the first Tudor King!
TILNEY:	We are in uncertain times now. Our Queen has steered the ship of state for so long, that many cannot imagine anyone else at the helm, but one day there must be a new Captain, and our Queen has supplied no young sailors. My God! Did I just wish the Queen's death? That is treason! I must be mad!
	[*Shaken* TILNEY *pours himself some wine, and as an afterthought fills* SHAKESPEARE's *goblet*]
SHAKESPEARE:	No, Sir Edmund you are right, there is none to succeed her, unless it be the Earl of Essex who flatters her that she is still young and fair.
TILNEY:	You don't want to listen to gossip about the vexed problem of the succession, and neither should you forget your place in the Great Chain of Being. You are a common player and sometime writer. But we are in unchartered waters.
SHAKESPEARE:	Then perhaps we must learn how to navigate this ship together.
TILNEY:	Little did I realise I was addressing the Queen's new Admiral! Stick to writing if I were you. So back to the "lamentable Tragedy of King

Richard the Third" here you describe the Crookback as "tyrannous in authority", very good! We will make a writer fit for Royal patronage out of you yet.

[TILNEY *turns the page*]

No. I spoke too soon. On the very next page what do you write? "Enter a murderer his name is Will Slaughter". Will Slaughter? Really?

SHAKESPEARE: It was but a foolish jest.

TILNEY: I fail to see the joke.

SHAKESPEARE: It was a thing that Kit Marlowe and Tom Kyd would do – write outrageous names into the foul copy of the script before sending it to the Office of the Revels.

TILNEY: Why?

SHAKESPEARE: To make you and your clerks laugh.

TILNEY: It would appear that too has failed. And what have we here? A funny French courtier! How original! The French King will split his sides laughing at that before he has you beheaded. The death of Richard at Bosworth Field? There needs to be much more blood, oh and maybe we can see him buried under the carts?

[TILNEY *puts down the quill and sits back. Unaware that* SHAKESPEARE *is seething quietly*]

This playscript will not do. I cannot approve it. Do you not know the great historian Sir Thomas More?

SHAKESPEARE: Yes I do. The last time I was in this office was when I came to deliver the play "Sir Thomas More" – which you then banned.

TILNEY: I felt it encouraged attacks on foreigners, so I requested ...

[TILNEY *goes to a file or ledger*]

"leave out the insurrection wholly, begin with Sir Thomas More as Mayor of London, report on his good service ... the mutiny against the Lombards, only by a short report NOT otherwise **at your own peril**".

[SHAKESPEARE *helps himself to another wine*]

SHAKESPEARE: Did you even read it? I did not attack foreigners but had Thomas More defend them.

TILNEY: I am surprised you even wished to write a play about a man who wanted us to remain tied to Rome. Now instead the House of Tudor have allowed us to take back control of our church.

SHAKESPEARE: It was a story that made for good theatre, that is all. More never knew Richard, but in Stratford I heard some still call him the King of the North.

TILNEY: I don't care if they call him the Queen of the Fairies that is not what Her Majesty wants.

SHAKESPEARE: Perhaps Sir Edmund, as you have such an image of what the Queen wants you should write it yourself?

TILNEY: I do write. But I write learned books.

SHAKESPEARE: Learned books? You have written a learned book? I should very much like to see this learned book.

TILNEY: Would you? Well by good fortune, I still have copies here, they did not sell as well as my publisher believed they would.

[*he hands a book over his table*]

SHAKESPEARE: "A brief and pleasant discourse of the duties in marriage called the flower of friendship" – well that title really trips off the tongue.

TILNEY: I do not write for lewd and common persons, but for Lords and Ladies, the Privy Council.

[SHAKESPEARE *fans and flicks through the pages*]

SHAKESPEARE:	You could certainly use this in the Privy.
TILNEY:	How dare you! I have devised great courtly revels for Kings and Queens, who hold me in high esteem, a thing of which you can only dream.
SHAKESPEARE:	Ooh some poetry there Sir Edmund! I dream of Kings and Queens, great Lords and Ladies too, but I know them, I make them in my mind and put them upon the stage for all to meet.
TILNEY:	There is a vast difference between meeting them in your mind and meeting them at Court.
SHAKESPEARE:	A book on marriage? And yet your own wife has been wed four times! This could be considered hypocrisy from its writer, could it not?
TILNEY:	What mean you?
SHAKESPEARE:	Your wife, Dame May, you are her fourth husband are you not? She gets through them doesn't she? Like a fire ship through the Armada, you want to watch her!
TILNEY:	I would make that your last goblet of wine if I were you.
	[but SHAKESPEARE continues to drink becoming more careless in his talk]
SHAKESPEARE:	I want this play to show another facet of Richard of Gloucester from the one I showed in Harry Sixth.
TILNEY:	Why?
SHAKESPEARE:	That play was one of my first, I can do more with the character now he is King.
TILNEY:	Just do as More did with the King.
SHAKESPEARE:	Thomas More again? A good character for a play, but hardly impartial. It's obvious he wrote about Richard to flatter the King, but little good that did him. The King turned on More because

he wouldn't agree to him marrying Anne Boleyn – was she as lust inducing as they say I wonder? I heard she had six fingers, she would know how to pleasure a man ...

[SHAKESPEARE *makes a masturbating sign with his hand.* TILNEY *catches it and forces the goblet from his hand*]

TILNEY: You are aware that is the Mother of our Queen you speak of? I would wager you have never been to Hampton Court. I go there quite often in my position as Master of the Revels – and do you know the first thing I do when I get there?

SHAKESPEARE: Well it's a long journey from London, pay a visit to the Great House of Easement?

[TILNEY *taking him by the neck slams* SHAKESPEARE *against the wall*]

TILNEY: I go into the Great Hall and I look up at the roof, and there looking back at me are little wooden faces and I always study one in particular, I know that face like my own, they are the eavesdroppers, and they remind us that when we are at Court, or no matter where we are, the eye of the monarch is ever upon us.

[TILNEY *points to the portrait of Queen Elizabeth, he then drags* SHAKESPEARE *over to the fire and holds him uncomfortably close to it pushing his face towards the flames*]

How dare you swagger in here, Southampton's bum boy, and presume to offer me – The Master of the Revels – this pile of stinking dung!

[*He throws the script at* SHAKESPEARE]

An even bigger dung heap than the one your father was fined for piling up outside your Warwickshire hovel. It's cold out isn't it? Well, I can have a fire whenever I want, because I am

Master of the Revels, appointed by the monarch who is in turn appointed by God, so I am a lot closer to God then you are. Her Majesty is like this fire, if you are within her charmed circle you may feel the warmth of her favour upon you, but at present you are outside – in the cold – but the door is half open – you have barely one foot inside but if you keep your nose clean you may gain admittance to the Royal Court.

[*he releases* SHAKESPEARE]

Peace, the charms wound up.

[TILNEY *walks away equally shaken. He pours himself a goblet of wine.* SHAKESPEARE *rises to his feet. A long pause*]

SHAKESPEARE: Forgive me Sir Edmund, I don't know what came over me.

TILNEY: I do. Several large goblets of my finest wine.

SHAKESPEARE: I fear your fine wine went straight to my head, I have but little to eat since breakfast.

TILNEY: Why?

SHAKESPEARE: My credit not being good in London, mine host serves me no meat, truly these are my salad days ... literally, radishes for breakfast every day.

[TILNEY *discreetly wafts his handkerchief. Then pours* SHAKESPEARE *water from a pitcher*]

TILNEY: If you want meat Master Shakespeare, you need to learn how to dine with those in power. You need not worry about dining on radishes, not when I can ensure that you are one of the Queen's own players. You are still here Master Shakespeare? Should you not be writing?

SHAKESPEARE: I must leave London.

TILNEY:	Why?
SHAKESPEARE:	To see my wife and children for a brief visit.
TILNEY:	Now? Can this not wait?
SHAKESPEARE:	No, Sir Edmund. My father has made some unwise investments, and is in some debt, which I have had to use my receipts from the Box Keeper's office to help him. He has had to sell his properties and we all now reside in the small house in Henley Street.

[TILNEY *discreetly notes this down*]

TILNEY:	But surely you can see that a play commissioned by Her Majesty would help you and your family?
SHAKESPEARE:	You are too kind, Sir Edmund.
TILNEY:	No, just protecting my reputation as Master of the Revels. So, let us have no more talk about the "King of the North". Show me "The Crookback King". Make sure you take your quill and plenty of parchment. Oh and here is a travelling companion for you.

[TILNEY *hands* SHAKESPEARE *a book*]

Thomas More's biography of "Richard the Third", I have it because I am a historian not a heretic by the way.

[SHAKESPEARE *takes the book and bows*]

SHAKESPEARE:	My apologies again for my outspoken words, I am not a man to indulge in a debauch, you may ask my fellow player Christopher Beeston, if you wish.
TILNEY:	I have no intention of speaking to actors if I don't have to.
SHAKESPEARE:	Of course, good day Sir Edmund.

[TILNEY *dismisses him with a wave.*

SHAKESPEARE exits.

TILNEY picks up Shakespeare's address and reads it]

TILNEY: Henley Street, Stratford upon Avon.

[He walks to the door, opening it, he EXITS]

LIGHTS UP

SHAKESPEARE *enters having left the Revels office when a man appears in the darkness.* SHAKESPEARE *turns fearing robbery.*

A VOICE:	You there!
SHAKESPEARE:	What do you want?
A VOICE:	A commission from the Master of the Revels would be nice – Will.
	[*The man moves into the light, he is unkempt and his bandaged hands are gnarled and the fingers cannot move*]
SHAKESPEARE:	Tom? Thomas Kyd? Is that you?
KYD:	Aye Will, I thought these …
	[*he lifts his hands*]
	… would have told you. The handiwork of Richard Topcliffe, the result of being accused of blasphemy, I can no longer write with these, but I have still have this.
	[*he pulls out a dog-eared manuscript which he hands to* SHAKESPEARE]
SHAKESPEARE:	[*reads title*] "The Spanish Tragedy", Greatest and best of the revenge tragedies.
KYD:	I've revised it, I tried to get to see Tilney to have him licence it, I saved up the money, but his Yeoman would not allow me in, he threw me out into the street.
SHAKESPEARE:	I am sorry Tom. It is a magnificent work.
KYD:	It's good, isn't it Will? I love every character in it, the swaggering sadist Pedringano, beautiful Bel-Imperia. Would Burbage have it for the Lord Chamberlain's Men?
SHAKESPEARE:	Tom, you know the play belongs to Henslowe,

it's not yours to offer.

[SHAKESPEARE *hands it back to* KYD]

KYD: But I wrote it!

SHAKESPEARE: For Henslowe! At the Rose! Tom you know the rules, we sell our plays to the playhouses, and they own them in perpetuity.

KYD: More like Purgatory! That's where I am.

SHAKESPEARE: If it were down to me, I would love to be in this.

KYD: Bugger off Will, you need good actors in this play.

[KYD *laughs and* SHAKESPEARE *smiles*]

SHAKESPEARE: Thank you for reminding me of my place in "the great chain of being". I am sorry Tom, since your arrest, your name bears the scars of infamy … ooh!

[SHAKESPEARE *writes this down*]

KYD: You think I don't know! Those I did call friends cross the street to avoid me, I passed the Rose the other day, Henslowe called out, he had some luckless lad emptying the privies into a bucket, "know the difference between you and a bucket of dung?" Henslowe shouts, "a bucket," he said, and laughed in my face.

SHAKESPEARE: I don't know what to say Tom.

KYD: "Can I help you?" might be a start.

SHAKESPEARE: What do you want?

KYD: Don't sound so enthusiastic!

SHAKESPEARE: I apologise but I wanted to be on Oxford Street by now, I must return home to Stratford to see my family.

KYD: Why bother? They've probably forgotten what you look like.

[SHAKESPEARE *takes* KYD's *hands, he screams in agony*]

SHAKESPEARE: My son died Tom.

[KYD *massages his hands*]

KYD: For the love of God Will, my hands! Mind you Greene's hands were so swollen by the end he could scarce hold a quill, of course that was the booze. Well, he's gone and I can't write any more, not with these.

SHAKESPEARE: What do you want Tom?

KYD: I have to move from my lodgings. I can no longer afford the rental, it is too large for me, besides it reminds me too much of living there with Kit.

SHAKESPEARE: I am sorry Tom; I know you and Marlowe were close.

KYD: You have no idea.

SHAKESPEARE: I think I do.

KYD: Of course, and how is "Grisly Risley" the darling of the playhouse boys?

SHAKESPEARE: I don't know, I haven't seen his Grace the Earl of Southampton for a long time.

KYD: He's probably got a new favourite these days, you're getting past it Will.

SHAKESPEARE: You really don't help yourself, do you Tom?

KYD: I am sorry Will, it's just that I need a hand – literally – to help me pack my few possessions, it's too difficult for me to pick things up.

SHAKESPEARE: Oh, very well.

KYD: Thank you Will – just this way.

[*lights up in another area strewn with pages of writing*]

SHAKESPEARE: Tilney would have a fit if he saw this mess.

KYD:	Aye Will.
	[*He mimics* TILNEY]
	This is all disordered, how can I register this?!
	[SHAKESPEARE *has picked up loose sheets*]
SHAKESPEARE:	Tom, this looks like Kit Marlowe's writing.
KYD:	It is.
SHAKESPEARE:	In God's name Tom why have you kept these? You were tortured for what you and Kit wrote before, they said it was blasphemy, burn it.
KYD:	I cannot.
SHAKESPEARE:	I know you have no fire.
	[*he picks up a bottle*]
	But I see you have spirits, douse them in that, then a spark from your tinder box will burn them.
	[KYD *takes the bottle but starts drinking from it. SHAKESPEARE looks at what he has in his hand*]
	Tom, this writing, "Moses is but a juggler", "Religion is to keep men in awe", "Protestants are hypocritical asses!" The only ass I see is not Nick Bottom, but Thomas Kyd! Did you think you could get away with this?
KYD:	That is Marlowe's.
SHAKESPEARE:	It's in your handwriting Tom!
KYD:	I copied it out for him, that is all.
SHAKESPEARE:	Really? You think they will believe that?
KYD:	Kit told me, he went to a place, with other men.
SHAKESPEARE:	Our patrons are not always as other men …
KYD:	No not like that, Kit would go to meet with great men, he told me Sir Walter Raleigh was there, it was called "The School of Night".
SHAKESPEARE:	And what did Sir Walter teach there may I ask?

	No don't tell me!
KYD:	Rational thought Will! Not superstition! The hidden mysteries of nature and science, the liberal arts, Kit said he could show sound reason for atheism.
	[SHAKESPEARE *points at* KYD's *hands*]
SHAKESPEARE:	I can see the Torturer Royal, Richard Topcliffe clearly had an open mind on the subject when he discoursed with you about it.
KYD:	I railed at Topcliffe, "Religion is a device of politic", I said.
SHAKESPEARE:	No, you didn't.
KYD:	What?
SHAKESPEARE:	You blamed everything on Marlow.
KYD:	Well, he didn't help himself either going around London telling everyone there was an extra devil on stage in "Dr Faustus", that Satan himself would be on stage at the Rose, which now you come to think of it, is pretty good marketing.
SHAKESPEARE:	[*still reading through paper*] "The Woman of Samaria and her sister were whores, and Christ laid more than his hand on them, Angel Gabriel was a pimp to the Holy Ghost" – do you want your hands cut off this time? Destroy this stuff now.
KYD:	No! they are all I have left of Kit – all we have left of our friend.
SHAKESPEARE:	I will speak plainly Tom. Kit Marlow had no need of enemies with a friend like you.
KYD:	What!
SHAKESPEARE:	I was told of the whining letters you sent after Kit's death, begging the Earl of Sussex and Lord Strange to be your patrons again, putting all the

blame on Kit, denying you wrote anything wrong.

KYD: Of course. You would never write anything wrong, would you? You who write plays you don't care about, to help in acquiring property that you do care about.

SHAKESPEARE: That's not true Tom! Yes, I want success but only to help restore my father's reputation and to provide for my family.

KYD: Some men do not have families and are not made to caper in ladies' chambers.

SHAKESPEARE: Like Richard the Third

[SHAKESPEARE *picks up another bundle of sheets and reads it*]

What is this? Talk of the Devil, "The True Tragedy of Richard of Gloucester", of course Kit, our idea that we worked on, before you were taken from us.

KYD: I loved Kit, God knows why, he was intemperate and of a cruel heart, and let me tell you Kit was stabbed in the back before he was stabbed in the eye, and who by? Your detractor, Robert Greene.

SHAKESPEARE: Kit thought Greene his friend.

KYD: Funny sort of friend, who described Kit's Tamburlaine as "Daring God out of Heaven with its blasphemy".

SHAKESPEARE: Tamburlaine was a long dead barbarian! He wasn't a Christian.

KYD: Greene didn't care, know what he called Kit? "The cobbler's son Machieval". That got Tilney and Topcliffe onto him, so let's hope the Queen likes your new play as they are harsh critics. What is it? Don't worry, I am not going to steal it.

[KYD *holds up his hands*]

KYD: I can hardly hold my pintle to make water let alone a quill to write.

SHAKESPEARE: The Queen would have a play about Richard the Third.

KYD: Of course, what a surprise, "my Grand Daddy saved you from the evil misshapen Dick, long live the Tudors", except they can't, can they? Because she's the last one, unless some of the rumours I hear are true, that she really likes the way your quill works, the way you dip it in her inkwell, splash the ink over her sheets then turn over and do the other side. There's many that think you are her young lover Will.

[SHAKESPEARE *takes the bottle from his hands*]

SHAKESPEARE: For the love of God be silent! You're drunk! Here take these coins, the writer of "the Spanish Tragedy" should not appear like this.

KYD: Thank you Master Shakespeare. I will take them, and in return give you some advice, make sure they like your Richard the Third play, because they fear the **true** "Spanish Tragedy", Catholicism returning to England along with Philip when Gloriana goes. Yes, I asked Lord Strange for his patronage again, but I didn't get it, why? Because someone had him poisoned. Strange was Catholic, did you know that? He was vomiting stuff that actually corroded the metal where it landed, left his body stinking to high Heaven. Now I have heard of Catholic guilt, but I don't think it gets you like that! So, let's hope you don't end up a stinking corpse, puking and rusting your landlady's poker. You do know what happened to Kit, don't you? Stabbed in a "tavern brawl?" That's bollocks! It wasn't a tavern, it was a respectable woman's house, that news they spread about Kit was fake, and you know who else was there? ...

[*a thuggish figure appears at a door an "INSTRUMENT"*]

INSTRUMENT: Thomas Kyd. You are to accompany me for cross examination by the Lords of the Star Chamber.

KYD: I have done nothing.

INSTRUMENT: Tell that to the Star Chamber – they have a mind to "scrape your conscience" – it's funny they say that under torture ... sorry, under close questioning, all sorts of sins come to light.

[*the* INSTRUMENT *sees* SHAKESPEARE *who has bundled the pages of* MARLOWE's *writing into his pack*]

What the hell are you doing here?

KYD: He kindly offered to help me move my poor possessions.

INSTRUMENT: I wasn't talking to you, arsehole.

SHAKESPEARE: As Master Kyd has said, I came to assist him move. Nothing more.

INSTRUMENT: Really?

[*he indicates the strewn papers*]

What's this shit everywhere, don't you have a housekeeper? Oh no, I forgot you and your bumboy roommate didn't like girls, here allow me.

[INSTRUMENT *starts going through the papers*]

KYD: What are you looking for?

INSTRUMENT: Blasphemy, sedition, treason, the sort of thing you writers churn out all the time.

SHAKESPEARE: These are but waste and idle papers ...

INSTRUMENT: If I was you, I would shut my mouth, and piss

off to that rat infested hole Stratford on Avon.

SHAKESPEARE: How did you ...?

INSTRUMENT: The sewer in which you reside being Henley Street I believe?

KYD: Just go Will. I'll be alright.

INSTRUMENT: Will you blasphemy boy? We'll see.

[*he sees* SHAKESPEARE *is leaving*]

Oi! Not so fast Scribbler, what you got in your man bag there?

SHAKESPEARE: A play that the Queen did bespeak.

INSTRUMENT: Let's have a look at it.

SHAKESPEARE: The play is for Her Grace, and is only for her eyes, and that of Her Master of the Revels, you should know that. Perhaps I will mention you at Court.

INSTRUMENT: Alright! Keep your hair on! What's it about?

SHAKESPEARE: The last Plantagenet King

INSTRUMENT: Sounds a bit boring. I liked your one "Tight arse".

SHAKESPEARE: "Titus", Titus Andronicus.

INSTRUMENT: Yeah, whatever. I liked the bit when that girl got done over, and they cut her tongue out, and cut her hands off, loads of blood, I like that, there'd better be loads of blood in your new play.

SHAESPEARE: Thank you, it's very useful for a writer to get feedback.

INSTRUMENT: [*still searching the strewn papers*] What we got here then? [*he starts to read*] "The Bible is no more than vain and idle stories", "The Virgin Mary is no better than she should be?", "Christ knew John the Baptist carnally" – you filthy blaspheming Godless bastard.

[INTRUMENT *strikes* KYD *a blow*]

	Going to sell these to Devil Worshippers, were you?
KYD:	I have as good a right as the Queen for coin.
INSTRUMENT:	Treason!
	[*he strikes* KYD *another blow*]
KYD:	I swear these are not mine and were shuffled with mine, which are Godly and full of love for our Queen. It was just an accident caused by writing in one chamber.
INSTRUMENT:	Lies!
	[*he strikes* KYD]
SHAKESPEARE:	For pity's sake, hasn't he suffered enough?
INSTRUMENT:	No! Thomas Kyd, I arrest you for the writing of vile, heretical conceits. Scribbler piss off to Henley Street.
KYD:	Will, thank you, look to your family, take care, remember the dead do not bite.
	[KYD *is removed by the* INSTRUMENT]
SHAKESPEARE:	Take care of yourself Tom.

LIGHTS UP

MISTRESS MONTJOY, SHAKESPEARE's LANDLADY, is tidying up SHAKESPEARE's *room which has been ransacked and talking aloud to herself.*

MONTJOY: Look at this mess, oh Master Shakespeare what has become of you? Your clothes torn and ruined, bits of your plays everywhere, the room invaded and roughed up by that – ruffian, calls himself an "instrument"? No better than a common swine. What right has he to ransack the room of a writer for the Lord Chamberlain's Men, said he was looking for a play of yours, and I said "you'll have to wait and see it at the playhouse like everyone else", "what playhouse?" he said, "they're all closed! Something to do with The Isle of Dogs", he said. "No players go there", I says, "away with you", I said, "Or I'll call the Constables". He just laughed in my face he did, such a pig. "The Constables bow to me", he says and just laughed again.

[*footsteps are heard on the stairs*]

God preserve us, he has returned, he said he would, oh Master Shakespeare.

[*enter SHAKESPEARE, the relieved MISTRESS MONTJOY hurls herself at him and hugs him*]

SHAKESPEARE: Mistress Montjoy, have a care, we are both married, and I have not long departed my dear wife's bed.

MONTJOY: Oh Will! Thank God you're back, we have had a terrible visitation from the Master of the Revels.

SHAKESPEARE: Sir Edmund Tilney did this?

MONTJOY:	No! He said he came FROM the Master of the Revels, said he was looking for a play.
SHAKESPEARE:	Did he now?
MONTJOY:	Are you late with it Will? He was in a terrible temper, I couldn't stop him, he was throwing things everywhere. Are you in some sort of trouble? I keep an honest house here, not a bawdy house, I obey the curfew, I admit no swaggerers. All the neighbours have been gossiping, especially that Puritan bitch across the way, and Will, he said he's coming back.
SHAKESPEARE:	What did he look like?
MONTJOY:	Like the Devil himself, and he kept going on about your friend Ben Jonson, and the Isle of Dogs, I says to him, "Will Shakespeare don't go there. none but villains do", and now all the playhouses ...
SHAKESPEARE:	Isle of Dogs? What about the playhouses?
MONTJOY:	They're all shut Will – all of them, on Tilney's orders he said.
SHAKESPEARE:	Oh God. Ben what have you done?
	[*footsteps are heard running up the stairs and* INSTRUMENT *is heard singing*]
INSTRUMENT:	"You traitors all that do devise To hurt our Queen in treacherous wise And in your hearts do still surmise Which way to hurt our England" [*"England" is said like a football chant*]
MONTJOY:	Will! he's back!
	[*the door is thrown open and the thuggish* INSTRUMENT *stands there,* MONTJOY *screams*]
INSTRUMENT:	Hello again Scribbler
	[INSTRUMENT *turns to* MONTJOY]
	Shut your row strumpet! or I'll shut it for you.

[*he produces a dagger*]

Nice time in the countryside Scribbler? Your daughter's not bad is she? I know she's getting on a bit now, must be what? Over 20? But I definitely would.

[*he thrusts his hips crudely*]

Well it's back to work now, someone wants a play from you.

SHAKESPEARE: If you are from the Office of the Revels, they may want to reconsider their recruitment practices.

INSTRUMENT: Work for "on the take Tilney"? Not me Scribbler! Richard Topcliffe is my guvnor.

MONTJOY: Oh God Will! That's the torturer, you told me what he done to your friend Kyd.

INSTRUMENT: Kyd got what he deserved.

[*the INSTRUMENT mimes crippled hands*]

You want to meet my friend, slut?

[*he shows her the dagger*]

Just like the one that pervert met, what was his name? – liked tobacco and boys apparently, and if you ask me, they certainly damaged his health!

[SHAKESPEARE *starts as he recognises this crude description of his friend*]

SHAKESPEARE: Marlowe, Christopher Marlowe.

INSTRUMENT: That's him, filthy bastard, wrote poncey poems, I could do better than that shit.

[*he goes up to* MONTJOY]

Here you are Slut, "come live with me and be my whore, and you can beg from door to door".

[MONTJOY *strikes the* INSTRUMENT *across the face with a powerful blow, he reels and clutches*

	his face in agony]
MONTJOY:	I am not a slut. I am a married woman.
INSTRUMENT:	You take money from a common player, and therefore you are a slut, strumpet.
MONTJOY:	I take money for his keep, nothing more.
SHAKESPEARE:	Why do you not fetch this gentleman some of that fine spirit you keep downstairs?
	[SHAKESPEARE *nods to indicate she should leave*]
INSTRUMENT:	I say who stays and who leaves. Looks after you, doesn't she Scribbler? What a fine fire. Now about this play ...
	[*he picks up a script*]
	What's this one? "Love's Labour's Won"? Sounds like a right load of old bollocks.
	[*he throws it on the fire*]
SHAKESPEARE:	That was the foul copy.
INSTRUMENT:	Very foul! It stinks.
SHAKESPEARE:	It's the only one! You have no right to come in here.
INSTRUMENT:	Oh, I have every right!
	[*he picks up another script*]
	And what have we here Scribbler?
	[*He reads it out haltingly*]
	"Car-de-nio". We don't want that foreign rubbish.
	[*he throws it on the fire*]
	Where's your English play, Richard the Third?
	[*he capers around like a hunchback*]
SHAKESPEARE:	I told you, I have it here.
	[*he pats his pack*]

So there was no need to do that.
[SHAKESPEARE *points at the fire*]

INSTRUMENT: Another foul copy was it? Mind you my Master says all your work smells like shit, Scribbler.

MONTJOY: He is not a Scribbler.

INSTRUMENT: If my Master says you are a Scribbler, then you are a Scribbler, Scribbler. Isn't that right slut?

[*he capers up and menaces her as Richard III at the same time* SHAKESPEARE *picks up a book but the* INSTRUMENT *turns suspecting* SHAKESPEARE *is getting a weapon*]

What are you up to Scribbler?

SHAKESPEARE: Sir Edmund loaned me this book, Thomas More's biography of Richard the Third.

[SHAKESPEARE *hands it to him*]

INSTRUMENT: What sort of a idiot do you take me for? You think I just come out of Bedlam? You telling me the Master of the Revels would give you a book written by some Catholic arsehole after that nonce in Rome called our Queen a bastard and excomplicated er … excunterated …

SHAKESPEARE: Excommunicated.

INSTRUMENT: I KNOW! And I ain't here to carry your bleeding book.

[*he drops it hard on* SHAKESPEARE's *foot*]

Ooh aren't I a butterfingers?! Carry it your bleeding self.

[SHAKESPEARE *picks it up and puts it on the table by his bag, moving something inside the bag*]

INSTRUMENT: Now what you doing?

SHAKESPEARE: Just making sure I have another quill, should I need to do some fresh scribbling for your master.

INSTRUMENT: Excellent idea Scribbler. Oh, and by the way
                 Strumpet, I was never here, so don't let me
                 hear it from your gossips.

                 [*he shows her the dagger*]

                 Come, my Master grows impatient.

SHAKESPEARE: Don't want to keep a theatre lover waiting, do
                 we?

SHAKESPEARE *and* INSTRUMENT *exit.*

MISTRESS MONTJOY *slumps to the floor.*

BLACKOUT

LIGHTS UP

Back in the Revels Office

SHAKESPEARE *and* TILNEY *are on.*

TILNEY: First I must apologise for your "escort". He is a rough and uncultured fellow.

SHAKESPEARE: Uncultured is true, he has just thrown two of my unseen works on the fire.

TILNEY: A mere trifle. I am sure by next week you will have replaced them with more plays. But those are not the plays we are here to talk about.

SHAKESPEARE: A moment if I may Sir Edmund? In between calling me "Scribbler" and poking me with his dagger, my escort mentioned he works not for you, but for Richard Topcliffe, he is the torturer is he not?

[from the hidden door RICHARD TOPCLIFFE *enters, charming, urbane, but a complete psychopath, the balance of power changes as* TILNEY *is immediately subservient to* TOPCLIFFE]

TOPCLIFFE: Oh dear, "torturer" is such an ugly word, Do you not find it an ugly word Sir Edmund?

[the terrified TILNEY *nods]*

TILNEY: Indeed Master Topcliffe.

TORCLIFFE: And I thought you to be a poet Master Shakespeare! I prefer to say "enforcer" and I am an artist too, and as your instrument is the quill, mine is the rack, the thumbscrew and the red-hot irons, I worked their magic on Thomas Kyd.

[he produces a small black notebook]

See I have him in my little black book, I like to

keep a record of all the famous people I meet, otherwise you lose track of whom you rack, don't you? Yes! Here is "Thomas Kyd". I have ticked it and written "I racked him", actually I used my special rack that I keep in my house. I designed it myself, so much better than those common racks at the Tower, it dislocates the joints to perfection. He soon informed on his roommate, and bedfellow too no doubt, Christopher Marlowe, that he had written blasphemous and seditious material.

SHAKESPEARE: Marlowe wrote wonderful material and Kyd's hands were destroyed, he could not write again.

TOPCLIFFE: What are you complaining about? One less rival for you I would have thought, I know you writers, in and out of each other's squalid lodgings, in and out of each other's beds, one moment carousing in taverns together, the best of friends, the next at each other's throats all accusing the other of stealing their work, but let us talk of more pressing matters such as ...

[TOPCLIFFE snaps his fingers, TILNEY hands SHAKESPEARE a playbook]

SHAKESPEARE: [reads cover] "The Isle of Dogs a satire by Ben Jonson".

[SHAKESPEARE starts to read the playbook]

TILNEY: Did you know about this seditious filth?

SHAKESPEARE: Er no, but it would appear to be quite a challenging piece of work ...

TOPCLIFFE: It's treason, that's what it is. It makes a mockery of all the Privy Council.

SHAKESPEARE: Really?

TILNEY: Making fun of politicians is not the role of the theatre.

TOPCLIFFE:	It makes a crude jest of the vexed problem of the succession, it may be that the throne passes to James of Scotland, maybe to the Earl of Essex, but one thing I do know, it's not going to pass to "Martin the Ape" from the bear baiting …
SHAKESPEARE:	I think that it's more likely to be a man dressed up.
TILNEY:	It doesn't matter! That's not the point, he has made fun of the Emperor of Russia, calling him a reed that bends with the wind, it will utterly mar all our trade into that country.
TOPCLIFFE:	We cannot afford to upset the Russians. And even worse, he called the King of Poland a pole.
SHAKESPEARE:	Well, he is.
TILNEY:	Not that kind of Pole, a "pole"!
	[*he mimes an erect penis*]
SHAKESPEARE:	I can see how this work would cause some upset in London.
TOPCLIFFE:	In London? The Polish ambassador has demanded a meeting with the Queen, the troublesome stir which has happened about this, is a great rumour that hath filled all England.
SHAKESPEARE:	Since when?
TOPCLIFFE:	Since your friend Jonson penned and performed these obnoxious scribblings taken from the devil's own book. The "Isle of Dogs", is I understand a notorious hideaway for villains, they actually compare politicians with criminals.
SHAKESPEARE:	Shocking!
TILNEY:	You are sure you had no knowledge of this treasonable scrawl?
SHAKESPEARE:	Sir Edmund my time has been taken up with

	researching and writing the Crookback King. I have had no time to read other writers' work.
TILNEY:	There is a mighty commotion about this, I am ordered to close all playhouses till further notice – that will please the wherrymen with no fares to ferry people across to Bankside.
SHAKESPEARE:	It is not right to rob honest workmen of their living just to make a point. Let me speak to Ben, he is oft times impetuous but I shall go and see him about this foolhardy play and make him see the error of his ways.
TOPCLIFFE:	And which tavern will Master Jonson be drinking in today, I wonder?
SHAKESPEARE:	He drinks in several.
TOPCLIFFE:	Oh, we know.

[TOPCLIFFE *brings out his book and checks information*]

But you won't find him in his favourite, "The Mermaid", nor "The Boars Head" where he keeps his whore, Ben Jonson can go to "the Devil" or rather he can't, not because he has exhausted his credit there, like he has so oftentimes before, but because he now has a new place to sup, but I fear he will find the bill of fare somewhat limited there, bread and water to be precise, you see Ben Jonson now resides in the Marshalsea Prison.

[*a long pause*]

SHAKESPEARE:	Is there any solution to this problem that I may be the instrument of?
TOPCLIFFE:	How kind of you Master Shakespeare to offer to be of service. And talking of instruments, my band of "instruments", all men who have seen tough service for Queen and Country, will be paying a visit to the Marshalsea, so finally Ben

	Jonson will be equal to Thomas Kyd, his hands will be crushed and he will never write again.
TILNEY:	Not that there will be anywhere to write for, as I am ordered your playhouses are all to be pulled down.
SHAKESPEARE:	Is there a way out of this?
TILNEY:	Where there's a Will there's a way!
TOPCLIFFE:	But Will, where is "The True History of Richard the Third"? For that is the key that will release Master Jonson from his lodgings in the Marshalsea and send my "instruments" back their lodging at the Tower. Do we understand each other Master Shakespeare?
SHAKESPEARE:	I have what you require. And it will free Master Jonson?
	[SHAKESPEARE *goes to hands over a script but drops it, he makes great play of picking it up – he also takes the opportunity to place loose pages within it. He goes to hand it to* TOPCLIFFE *who looks at it with disdain*]
TOPCLIFFE:	I do not soil my hands with playhouse material, especially when it has been on the floor of a clerk's office.
	[*he snaps his fingers imperiously*]
	Tilney!
	[TILNEY *takes it and reads the front cover*]
TILNEY:	"The tragedy of King Richard the Third, containing his treacherous plots against his brother Clarence, the pitiful murder of his innocent nephews, his tyrannical usurpation with the whole course of his detested life and his most deserved death".
SHAKESPEARE:	I made him a hunchback, just like Robert Cecil, the Spymaster's son.

	[*pause while* TOPCLIFFE *decides how to take this*]
TOPCLIFFE:	Excellent Master Shakespeare, I knew we would understand each other. Oh, there's just one more thing, the chill air of treason is still upon this room and we must burn it out.
	[TOPCLIFFE *gets* TILNEY *to hand* SHAKESPEARE *the "Isle of Dogs" script*]
	If you be so good as to throw this filth upon the fire, we may have full resolution.
SHAKESPEARE:	As a writer yourself Sir Edmund, might you not spare the work of a fellow artist?
TILNEY:	How dare you compare my musing upon the blessed institution of marriage, with these depravities?
	Sodom.
TOPCLIFFE:	Quite right Sir Edmund …
TILNEY:	[*plowing on*] And Gomorrah, had they playhouses even they would hesitate to show such scenes, into the fire with it Master Shakespeare!
	[SHAKESPEARE *throws "Isle of Dogs" on the fire*]
TOPCLIFFE:	The ship of state must not run aground on the "Isle of Dogs". Now on a brighter note it is time for "The greatest villain on the English stage" Sir Edmund, this is your matter I believe.
	[*TOPCLIFFE exits*
TILNEY:	[*potters around preparing props and costumes singing to himself*]
	"Consider what the end will be Of traitors all in their degree Hanging is still their destiny That trouble the peace of England"

[*running out of hands he absent-mindedly drops a black wig onto* SHAKESPEARE's *head, who doesn't notice but continues to stare into the fire*]

Tableaux to End Act 1: SHAKESPEARE *looks into the fire hunched over and wearing the wig he has the essence of the Crookback King.*

BLACKOUT

ACT 2 – 1603

As lights go up, TILNEY *walks to the portrait of* ELIZABETH. *He turns it in a matter of fact way, on the back is a portrait of* JAMES I. *Bored, he raises his hand and takes his oath in a monotone with no meaning*

TILNEY: I, Sir Edmund Tilney do agree to accept the office of Master of the Revels and the duties of that high station will undertake to the best of my skill and ability. I swear to be a true and faithful servant to our Sovereign Lord, King James of England, Scotland, and France. I will serve the King as Master of the Revels and as Examiner for all plays or any other entertainment of the stage whatsoever. I will know nothing hurtful or prejudicial to His Majesty's Royal Person, Crown or Dignity but I shall reveal all to the Lord Chamberlain.

[*From behind the portrait* KING JAMES I *emerges **(played if possible by the Elizabeth performer)**, with a goblet of wine in his hand, tipsy, with his lolling tongue, rolling eyes and slobbering mouth*]

JAMES: So, Sir Edmund, you are going to reveal all to my Lord Chamberlain are you? I shall await that with interest! I said to the Lord Chamberlain when he said I had to "show myself to the people", I said, "God's wounds! Shall I pull down my breeches and they can see my arse?"

[JAMES *laughs uproariously – there is an awkward pause*]

TILNEY: Very droll Your Majesty. I trust Your Majesty had a pleasant progress from Scotland? How do you find England?

JAMES:	Well you just leave Scotland and it's lying there like a turd!
	[JAMES *laughs uproariously and pours more wine*]
	I "find" England looks a hell of a lot better after a goblet or two of French wine!
	[JAMES *goes to offer* TILNEY *the second goblet, gets carried away and pours it into his first wine*]
TILNEY:	I understand you knighted over 100 men en route?
JAMES:	Aye I did, and a pig.
TILNEY	A pig?
JAMES;	I'd been bevvying you Ken?
TILNEY:	No Sire. **Edmund**! Sir Edmund Tilney.
JAMES:	"Ken" means "you know", you had better start to learn your Scottish Sir Edmund. Aye and I charge them thirty English pounds a go for a knighthood, and every little helps you ken?
TILNEY:	[*still can't follow or understand the King's Scottish slurred speech but thinks he is ingratiating himself*] Oh, och aye Your Majesty.
JAMES:	Are you taking the piss?
TILNEY:	[*out of his depth again*] I am not your physician Your Majesty, is this a bad time? I can return later.
JAMES:	I am no havin' them playhouse writers tek the pi...the rise outa me, ye ken? That's why I kept in the bit in your oath about you being "Examiner" of plays. Plus you get to read all the dirty plays, so that's a perk isn't it? You see some of those playwrights, they think to make fun of the Scots, Ben Jonson has just tried that with "Eastward Ho!"

TINLEY:	Oh God, not Jonson again!
JAMES:	How did that one get past you?
TILNEY:	I cannot think how that happened Your Majesty.
JAMES:	Well I suggest you try to, Sir Edmund, after all you are Master of the Revels are you not? He suggested all Scotsmen at the Court bugger off to the New World, and then said we all live together in "notorious cohabitation" defying marriage.
TILNEY:	Ah! Now Your Majesty, you are speaking my language ...
JAMES:	How dare you! I speak English as good as you, better in fact ...
TILNEY:	No, Your Majesty, I mean the sacred state of marriage, I know a thing or two about it, having written a book about it, allow me to present you with a copy, I still have many left ...
	[*he hands over yet another huge book*]
JAMES:	What's this? A doorstop? I don't want that.
	[JAMES *discards it,* TILNEY *looks crestfallen*]
TILNEY:	Your Majesty I am sure that the fine Scottish folk with whom you filled up ... er packed ... er graced the Court with since your glorious accession, would not live in matrimonial engagement without formal ceremony.
JAMES:	They would actually, some right reprobates some of them ye ken? But that's not the point, the point is, Ben Jonson can shove it "Eastward Ho" up his arse!
TILNEY:	I will have the play banned at once Your Majesty.
JAMES:	That has already been done.
TILNEY:	But that was my role, who has banned it?

JAMES:	The Lord Chamberlain, it would seem he has his eye on your job as Examiner of Plays.
TILNEY:	[*sotto voce*] He is welcome to it! [*aloud*] Very well Your Grace, I will have Jonson brought to the Office of the Revels and commence an investigation.
JAMES:	[*sarcastic*] That will terrify him. There are those who say that he should have his ears cut off and nose slit open.
TILNEY:	May I be so bold as to enquire who say this?
JAMES:	The Lord Chamberlain.
TILNEY:	Of course!
JAMES;	And my Courtiers.
TILNEY:	The Scottish ones?
JAMES:	Of course.
TILNEY:	Of course! I can assure you I will throw the book at Jonson over this Your Grace.
JAMES:	[*indicating* TILNEY's *book*] You may use your one, for I have no use for it. And I hope you have a far reach to throw it, for Jonson is in Marshalsea Prison.
TILNEY:	Oh no not again! I May I suggest you leave him there permanently this time?
JAMES:	I canna do that, I actually like him, he's a good drinking companion ye ken? He can drink me under the table, and that's saying something, and he's no lickspittle, it's just he'd have an argument in an empty chamber! He has greatly angered my favourite courtier, by his anti Scottish stuff, he has a scene where all the Scots take ship for the New World, but get drunk and crash it on the Isle of Dogs
TILNEY:	Not the Isle of Dogs again! He's obsessed!
JAMES:	So, I'll let him cool his heels in gaol for a few

weeks, you see Sir Edmund I see myself as a "One Nation" Monarch.

TILNEY: Well of course technically you are Monarch of two nations? Or three with Ireland, four if you count France.

JAMES: Don't quibble Tilney.

TILNEY: No, Your Grace. Leaving aside Jonson in what would appear to be his second home, the Marshalsea, if I may ascertain how the Revels Office may be at your service? For example, Her late Majesty ...

[JAMES *breaks wind noisily*]

JAMES: Better oot than in! Did you know if you don't fart regularly you get a "mazed brain"?

TILNEY: How fascinating Your Grace. As I was saying, Her late Majesty found it more financially prudent not to keep a permanent company of players but to pay for performances at Court as and when she wanted them.

JAMES: And they say us Scots are mean! No, none of that. I will have my own Men, what was that one she liked? The big fat funny boozer?

TILNEY: Francis Bacon?

JAMES: No! Falstaff that's him, Sir John Falstaff.

TILNEY: May I point out he is not a real person Your Majesty but just a playbook character ...

JAMES: I know that! I may be called "the wisest fool in Christendom" but I am not a idiot! Who's the Sassenach who wrote it?

TILNEY: William Shakespeare Your Majesty.

JAMES: That's the one, he's good, does he have a company?

TILNEY: He is a sharer in the Lord Chamberlain's Men, Your Grace.

JAMES:	Sod that! The Lord Chamberlain has enough to do, he doesn't need a company of Players, they will be my Men, The King's Men.
TILNEY:	As Your Majesty pleases.
JAMES:	So get them ready, I want them at my Coronation Procession, it will be good for me to be seen with arty-farty famous actors and such, and I want them looking presentable, I don't want them with their arses hanging out of their breeches ... at least not until the party later!

[TILNEY *is lost for words*]

JAMES:	So give them four yards of scarlet cloth each, that should do.
TILNEY:	Scarlet cloth Your Majesty?
JAMES;	Yes. Is there a problem Sir Edmund?
TILNEY:	It's just that the sumptuary laws as amended by the late King Henry the Eighth ...
JAMES:	I don't give a shit about rules made up by that lardy arsed church basher, what the hell does it matter what people wear?
TILNEY:	The feeling was that it helped people to know their place in the Great Chain of Being ...
JAMES:	The what? Oh, don't talk bollocks Tilney, that went out when those bloody Tudors exited the stage, I know some lovely sailor lads, they traverse the known world with their gallant crews of merry mariners, the taste of salty spume upon their lips ...

[TILNEY *does a double take*]

They discover unknown lands, and bring back exotic riches to enhance the prestige of the Kingdom, and, let's be honest, enrich the Royal coffers, so if they want some nice clothes what is wrong with that?

TILNEY:	Nothing Your Majesty.
JAMES:	Oh shit!
TILNEY:	Your Majesty?
JAMES:	Am I supposed to give my actors stuff? Old clothes and things?
TILNEY:	Well the tradition is that when a nobleman tires of his clothes or they grow out of fashion he passes them to his servants, they being forbidden to wear them by the Sumptuary Laws …
JAMES:	Which I think I just repealed …
TILNEY:	The servants sell the clothes to the playhouses. As long as the actors only wear them on stage, they need not fear arrest.
JAMES:	Arrest? Is that not a trifle excessive?
TILNEY:	The feeling is that all must know their place. I recall having to legislate in the matter of an actor playing a King at the Rose, who in his haste to reach the tavern after the performance went there wearing the King's robes, and was fined £20.
	[JAMES *laughs uproariously and goes to offer* TILNEY *wine then pours into his own goblet*]
JAMES:	The King drinking in the tavern! I would have paid his fine just to see such a thing. Why was I not told about the clothes thing? They could have had all those old clothes I found in that Jewel House, bugger all sparkly things in there, just loads of old rags, I ordered them to be cast out …
TILNEY:	Your Majesty that was the Royal Wardrobe! Clothes accumulated since the time of the sainted Edward the Confessor!
JAMES:	No bugger tells me anything! Well, some of

	them may still be out by the coal yard, in fact I saw one of the pages, wearing one of the dresses yesterday, nice boy, for a minute I thought I had had one too many, I thought Mad Lizzie had come back from the grave for me!
TILNEY:	Will Your Majesty wish to address Master Shakespeare and your new players as did the late Queen?
JAMES:	What the hell for? Just tell them their duties, I don't want to talk to them, they're actors, they will be happy to know they get free food and drink when they perform here. Talking of which, my Brother in Law the King of Denmark is coming over, I require entertainment.
TILNEY:	Of course Your Majesty, I understand Master Shakespeare has a play relating to Denmark, that should make your most Royal Brother in Law feel at home, it's probably a nice cheerful story about a happy Danish family ...
JAMES:	He will nae listen tae a play! He'll be soused by suppertime, plus I am not made of money you know, do me a masque, that's cheap isn't it? Oh, and he'll have all his Danish pals with him, so some nice looking lassies please, preferably with big diddies.
TILNEY:	Your Majesty! Women? On stage? That is most irregular, it is more usual to have boys.
JAMES:	Oh well I wouldn't want to break with some traditions, let's have some pretty boys as well, I will trust you to pick them.
	[JAMES gives TILNEY a wink]
TILNEY:	Of course Your Majesty, but regarding boys, may I be so bold as to point out ...
JAMES:	You are still here Sir Edmund? Should you not be preparing a masque? Give us the Queen of

Sheba, she would be a fair one for some pumping, I don't mind you licensing reasonable recreation for honest people but be warned I will brook no treason.

BLACKOUT

LIGHTS UP

Back in the Revels Office.

SIR EDMUND TILNEY *is with* SHAKESPEARE *who wears his scarlet suit from the Coronation.*

TILNEY: Master Shakespeare, welcome, I see your Coronation scarlet cloth was delivered, I am not sure it is necessary to wear it all the time.

SHAKESPEARE: I would not wish to commit any breach of etiquette, but I believe as a King's Man …

TILNEY: A Royal servant!

SHAKESPEARE: I say again a King's Man, we are both Royal servants, and as such should wear livery, is yours at the laundry?

TILNEY: Be that as it may, you have now received more new honours and responsibilities, no longer the Lord Chamberlain's Men, you are now The King's Men. You will give a play at court once a month, at Royal feasts and occasions, and you will be seen less by the Public in General, as befits Players privy to Court and the person of His Majesty.

SHAKESPEARE: Sir Edmund, I am loath to give up playing at the Globe, for if we do not do a play we do not get any pay, and I cannot live on the proceeds of one play a month at court, I have a family to support, and I do not forget our loyal audience at the Globe, they give their hard won pennies, to see the traffic of the stage, and let us be honest, the fat merchant with his buxom young wife, he will never be invited to see a play at Court, but he may spend three pennies and sit in the Middle Galleries, and see such stuff as dreams are made of. And knowing the gallants

	applaud good swordsmanship, we have the best swordsmen, and should an imperfect actor forget his part, they can look up and see what nobility sit above the players in the Lords Boxes. No! there is nowhere like the great Globe itself, and I will not give up our loyal audience, no disrespect to the great honour you do me.
TILNEY:	Beshrew me, you are a difficult man Master Shakespeare. You should have been a businessman, rather than waste your time at the playhouse.
SHAKESPEARE:	I like the Globe and willingly would waste my time in it.
TILNEY:	Well I have little time to waste, the King would have a masque about the Queen of Sheba for the visit of his Brother in Law the King of Denmark.
SHAKESPEARE:	I have a play about the state of Denmark …
TILNEY:	And I did attempt to interest him in it Master Shakespeare, but the King would none of it, to be honest I think the pair of them have the attention span of a couple of carp in the Royal fishponds, if you would forgive me I have to return to the masque.
	[TILNEY *picks up a quill and begins to write*, SHAKESPEARE *wanders the room looking at things and reading parchment*]
	Sorry Master Shakespeare, they are yet to be licensed plays not yet to be seen, do you mind?
SHAKESPEARE:	Forgive me
	[TILNEY *returns to work,* SHAKESPEARE *sits*]
TILNEY:	Master Shakespeare, you are still here?
SHAKESPEARE:	Yes.
TILNEY:	Why?

SHAKESPEARE:	I am invited to dine with a nobleman later in this vicinity, it would be somewhat irksome for me to have to return to my lodgings and tedious to traverse back to here like a travelling player. Those days are over for me now. I am wondering if I may prevail upon your kindness to allow me to kill some time here.
TILNEY:	This is the Office of the Revels, not St Paul's open to all loiterers.
SHAKESPEARE:	[*pointing to the badge on his arm*] Surely for a King's Man?
TILNEY:	Oh, very well, but please remember some of us are working.
SHAKESPEARE:	I will be as silent as the grave. Not a mouse stirring.
	[TILNEY *resumes writing.* SHAKESPEARE *picks up a book and starts to smile, he giggles, snorts, titters and is soon laughing like a drain*]
TILNEY:	What is the matter with you! I swear you do this on purpose! What do you read?
SHAKESPEARE:	"Sejanus", Ben Jonson's Tragedy – Funniest thing he ever wrote!
TILNEY:	Master Jonson will not be writing anything again for some time, he again resides in The Marshalsea Prison for writing lewd, mischievous and unseemly plays. What ails you and Jonson, you always bite the hand that feeds you?
SHAKESPEARE:	Vaulting ambition, that does o'er leap itself.
TILNEY:	I beg your pardon?
SHAKESPEARE:	Impatience.
TILNEY:	Impatience doth become a dog, that's mad.
SHAKESPEARE:	Very good, Sir Edmund, but if you would compare us to dogs, myself and Ben Jonson,

	stand like greyhounds in the slips, impatient to be heard.
TILNEY:	If you talk of dogs, Jonson lifts his leg and pisses against the world.
SHAKESPEARE:	The world is changing Sir Edmund, men like Ben and I are from humble stock, but we are not content to stay within our place which the House of Tudor were so keen to imprison us in. We can write plays as good, if not better than those who went to university, we write so everyone can understand, and enjoy, not just those who sit up in the Gentlemen's boxes with their paintings of the classics upon the walls, applauding any reference to the Ancients. I write humour for the groundlings as well, and I see the gentry laugh at it too. And mistake me not, as good sons we honour our fathers, but we want more than they had, and through our imaginations we may get it, and in return give back to them who raised us. I got my father a coat of arms.
TILNEY:	Oh yes of course, they finally knuckled under at the College of Herald's did they? Probably got tired of being badgered by your "patrons".
SHAKESPEARE:	I am more pleased for my good father John, who did the best for me, gave me an education that was as good as can be, and I have missed for nothing by not idling and spending all at university. Yes, I have bought the finest house in Stratford, but I do not forget where I have come from, and nothing gives me more pleasure than to sit in a small tavern, among the good folk I grew up with, an inkhorn about my neck, noting their honest plain talk. I feel at home there, I have a life there, which I will return to in a few years, I will not miss London or the playhouses when I am gone.

TILNEY:	I will never understand writers as long as I live. It was but a few years ago that you came to this very office with your play about the Crookback, the play that made you and Burbage thanks to my help. And back then Jonson was imprisoned for writing "Isle of Dogs", now we have "Eastward Ho" and Jonson back in gaol! He would appear to have learnt nothing! You both are like children, and I have little urge to act as your nursemaids.
SHAKESPEARE:	I should not worry. I have a feeling that all will work out well for Ben. It always has. That one was born under a lucky constellation
	[TILNEY *starts to write.* SHAKESPEARE *sidles over*]
SHAKESPEARE:	It is good to see you creating again Master Tilney. It puts me in mind of when we first met ....
	[TILNEY *cuts him off*]
TILNEY:	I am trying to create now Master Shakespeare.
	[SHAKESPEARE *hovers over* TILNEY *reading over his shoulder*]
	Do you mind?
SHAKESPEARE:	I beg your pardon.
	[*pause* – SHAKESPEARE *continues to lurk behind* TILNEY]
SHAKESPEARE:	"The Masque of The Queen of Sheba"! Interesting! Who did you say this is for?
TILNEY:	The King of Denmark.
SHAKESPEARE:	Oh! Really? Hmm.
TILNEY:	What is that supposed to mean?
SHAKESPEARE:	Nothing, I just heard something.
	[TILNEY *picks up his quill and tries to work, in a minute he puts it down*]

TILNEY:	Alright, out with it, what have you heard?
SHAKESPEARE:	Only that he is known as the most drunken Monarch in Christendom.
TILNEY:	What! To quote His Majesty, "No bugger tells me anything".
SHAKESPEARE:	I fear he may not have a mind to listen to anything for too long, and if I may give you some advice?
	[TILNEY *nods glumly*. SHAKESPEARE *points to a bit of script*]
	So here you have three Goddesses! And what are they called?
	[SHAKESPEARE *turns the page*]
	Faith, Hope and Charity. Bit dull, bit obvious.
TILNEY:	Do you think you could do any better?
SHAKESPEARE:	Well, yes, since you ask. Venus will please the lusty King of Denmark more than Faith, the ample breasted Juno will give more hope to the nobleman than Hope herself and the voluptuous Volupta will receive more donations from the Court than the Goddess Charity ever would. And there are some among the girls in the Stews who could be a very Goddess, or a Mermaid.
TILNEY:	[*looks up with a start*] The King has a mind for them to be played by the Ladies of the Court.
SHAKESPEARE:	Interesting. Maybe one day women will play upon the playhouse stages too.
TILNEY:	Don't be ridiculous Master Shakespeare. I did suggest that we use the Boys of the King's Men to play some parts, and he suggested that I choose them, he intimated he thought my interest in boys was less than professional.
	[SHAKESPEARE *stifles a laugh*]

SHAKESPEARE:	Of course, Sir Edmund, as The King's Men we will have two of our most charming and handsome boys to act as attendants on your Goddesses. I am sure those Court Ladies, your Goddesses, are even now eschewing the delights of Court to be ready for their roles. And if I may offer some more advice, make sure the masque is performed early in the evening, before both their Majesties start imbibing. When are you to perform?
TILNEY:	Ten at night.
SHAKESPEARE:	I see. All will be well on the night I am sure!
TILNEY:	Master Shakespeare, why not accompany me to the masque which I am to direct, and I warrant you will see, what could possibly go wrong?
SHAKESPEARE:	What indeed?
BLACKOUT	

LIGHTS UP

Drunken revelry and loud booing is heard.

SHAKESPEARE: It would appear the Jester you found is providing even less humour than the Morris Dancers.

[*a JESTER comes out with a Jester's hat flicking "V" signs and making angry obscene gestures at the unseen Royal audience*]

JESTER: Miserable bastards them Danes, ain't they?

SHAKESPEARE: Very!

[*the JESTER exits making rude gestures still*]

TILNEY: What time is it Master Shakespeare?

SHAKESPEARE: The iron tongue of midnight hath tolled already.

TILNEY: This is ridiculous! We have been here since six of the clock.

SHAKESPEARE: The King's Steward beckons Sir Edmund.

[TILNEY *indicates to the unseen Steward they are ready*]

TILNEY: Let us hope that Victory will cheer up the Court, Victory! Victory! Where is Victory when we need her?

[FEMALE PERFORMER *staggers on behind TILNEY as a drunken* VICTORY, *her helmet back to front and a cheap wooden sword in her hand.* SHAKESPEARE *indicates she is behind him.*

TILNEY *turning and mortified by what he sees,* VICTORY *swaying from side to side trying to focus*]

TILNEY: Is the lady drunk?

SHAKESPEARE: As a Lord.

TILNEY:	What!
SHAKESPEARE:	You would be far more victorious if your wings of Victory were pointing the right way.
	[SHAKESPEARE *puts her helmet the correct way round*]
VICTORY:	Where do I go now?
	[*without waiting for instructions she heads the wrong way*]
TILNEY:	That way! As you were told in rehearsals!
SHAKESPEARE:	Towards the crown.
VICTORY:	But there are two crowns unless I can see double.
TILNEY:	[*sotto voce*] You probably can.
SHAKESPEARE:	Towards the crown covered in jelly.
TILNEY:	Why the hell is the King of Denmark covered in jelly?
SHAKESPEARE:	It would appear the drunken Queen of Sheba upset the cake cart upon him!
TILNEY:	This is an outrage! These court ladies abandon their sobriety and roll about in drunkenness! Where is she? I will give her a piece of my mind.
SHAKESPEARE:	You will have to wake her up first.
	[*he points offstage where drunken snoring can be heard*]
TILNEY:	[*shouts into audience as if directing the masque*] Victory, mind the steps!
SHAKESPEARE:	Give him the sword.
VICTORY:	King James doesn't want it.
TILNEY:	Give it to the King of Denmark then.
VICTORY:	He doesn't want it either. Ooh he says he wants to give me his weapon.
TILNEY:	Come back here!

VICTORY:	He says he wants to dance with me.
TILNEY:	Get back here NOW!
VICTORY:	[*staggers back drunkenly*] What shall I do now?
TILNEY:	Go and sober up, and if you see Peace send her this way.
	[VICTORY *leaves*]
TILNEY:	Where are Faith, Hope and Charity?
SHAKESPEARE:	Drunk and spewing Sir Edmund.
TILNEY:	Well, it appears there is no hope then. My first Revel for King James is ruined!
SHAKESPEARE:	I hate to say "I told you so," but I did tell you that Venus, Juno and Volupta would have been more to the Danish King's liking.
TILNEY:	Well let's hope that Peace can save the day.
SHAKESPEARE:	And here comes Peace now!
	[*enter* PEACE *wearing a white robe, a blonde wig and angrily brandishing her olive branch. She is incandescent with rage!*]
PEACE:	I am SO ANGRY! I am incandescent with rage!
TILNEY:	Why?
PEACE:	[*starts to poke him with her olive branch*] I wanted to play the Queen of Sheba, why I am playing this total nonentity Peace? I haven't even got a nice costume. Do you know who I am?
TILNEY:	Peace?
PEACE:	My father knows the Lord Chamberlain.
TILNEY:	Yes, he would!
SHAKESPEARE:	Dear Lady, your natural beauty will provide a wondrous ornament to our most Royal Revels when you play the role of Peace for the Kings.
PEACE:	Well alright, what do I do?

SHAKESPEARE:	Just proceed now to the King.
PEACE:	Which one?
TILNEY:	Any one.
SHAKESPEARE:	Thank you Sir Edmund. Now offer the olive branch of peace with all modesty, stillness and humility.
	[PEACE exits. *We hear a scream offstage*]
SHAKESPEARE:	Give him the olive branch.
PEACE:	He says it doesn't want it.
SHAKESPEARE:	Give it to him anyway.
PEACE:	He says he wants to give it to me.
SHAKESPEARE:	Oh dear.
PEACE:	How dare you! No! I will not sit on your lap, you're covered in jelly, you dirty man, keep your hands to yourself you lascivious drunken sot! How dare you touch me again, take that!
TILNEY:	Don't hit him with the olive branch – it belongs to the Office of the Revels … too late.
PEACE:	And take that too, you foul drunken lustful maltworm.
SHAKESPEARE:	It would appear Sir Edmund that Peace hath made war upon Denmark.
	[PEACE *returns, her wig askew, covered in jelly, and with her olive branch broken*]
PEACE:	They really are rotten in the state of Denmark, aren't they?

She exits.

SHAKESPEARE *nods and reaches for his inkhorn to note this down*

BLACKOUT

LIGHTS UP

Back in the Revels Office, TILNEY *is packing away his scripts.*
SHAKESPEARE *enters.*

SHAKESPEARE: Good day Sir Edmund.

TILNEY: Come to gloat have you Master Shakespeare?

SHAKESPEARE: Gloat? I don't follow, and are the Office of the Revels moving?

TILNEY: No, but I may be, after that disastrous "Masque of The Queen of Sheba", I have had no communication from the Palace, other than …

[*he goes to his desk and checks a parchment*]

A request for Will Kempe to leap into the custard at Middle Temple.

SHAKESPEARE: Well it's money.

TILNEY: Oh, and a request for an actor to ride a giant fish up the Thames for a Royal Visit.

SHAKESPEARE: I am not sure who would want such an engagement?

TILNEY: The King has asked for Richard Burbage.

SHAKESPEARE: Tell him he will do it.

[*they both laugh*]

TILNEY: Do I detect you are settling an old score here Master Shakespeare?

SHAKESPEARE: Burbage is famous now since playing Richard the Third They all shout "Where's your horse?" when he enters the taverns.

TILNEY: Ah the fame of the Crookback King still follows him.

[*he reaches for the script of Richard III*]

SHAKESPEARE: [*interjecting quickly*] He takes all the lead roles

	for himself, I fear he would even take credit for writing the plays if he could.
TILNEY:	Surely your fame will outlive his? Players are ten a penny but writers are immortalised for ever.
	[*he reaches again for the script*]
SHAKESPEARE:	Allow me to explain Sir Edmund.
	[*lights change to the Globe.* SHAKESPEARE *has just finished reading Hamlet to the company,* BURBAGE *(autocratic leading man) stands*]
BURBAGE:	Excellent Will, thank you for reading to us your new play "Hamlet Prince of Denmark", and I am sure I speak for the whole company when I say what a pleasure it will be for me to play the role of the troubled Dane.
SHAKESPEARE:	A moment Richard, who am I to play in my own play?
BURBAGE:	The ghost I think.
SHAKESPEARE:	But surely I could play Rosencrantz?
BURBAGE:	That is marked down for Sly.
SHAKESPEARE:	Guildenstern?
BURBAGE:	Sinclair.
SHAKESPEARE:	Noble Horatio?
BURBAGE:	We have far more accomplished players in the company for that role.
SHAKESPEARE:	Well, how about I close the play as Fortinbras?
BURBAGE:	No Will! By that time you will be in the tiring house writing us your next play, what will you write for me next Will? I know, I would play a noble Moor next, you can do that for me, can't you?
SHAKESPEARE:	Richard I am no hired man, I am a Sharer in this company!

BURBAGE:	Yes Will, and you share your writing talent with us all. *Adieu, Adieu!* Sweet Prince, I have many of your fine lines to learn
SHAKESPEARE:	No mention of my acting talent then Richard?
	[*lighting indicates that we are back in the Revels Office*]
TILNEY:	It would appear Master Shakespeare that we are both men who – dare I say it – are underappreciated in our offices.
SHAKESPEARE:	I am sure that you can gain back the favour of King James.
TILNEY:	Really and how do you suggest I do that?
SHAKESPEARE:	What does the King like? Find that out and give it to him.
TILNEY:	Master Shakespeare, do you suggest I turn pimp or tavern keeper?
SHAKESPEARE:	I don't follow Sir Edmund.
TILNEY:	I will tell you what the King likes, the King likes nothing more than boys, the hunt, boys, getting drunk, boys oh and witchcraft.
SHAKESPEARE:	Aye there's the rub.
TILNEY:	Rubbing boys? I keep telling you I am not that way inclined …
SHAKESPEARE:	No! Witchcraft!
TILNEY:	Are you suggesting I risk my head in dabbling in the occult? And what do you know of witchcraft anyway?
SHAKESPEARE:	I know that the King fears witchcraft and yet is fascinated by it.
TILNEY:	Your informant is correct. His Majesty keeps the book "Hammer of the Witches" by his bed and has written a book called "Demonology".
SHAKESPEARE:	Has he indeed?

TILNEY:	Yes, But you did not answer my question Will – what do you know of witchcraft?
SHAKESPEARE:	"Secret black and midnight hags, within a circle of ancient standing stones, each one lays her choppy fingers upon her lips".
TILNEY:	What?
SHAKESPEARE:	In Stratford in Long Compton, my mother said there were witches there, that will be the opening of our play.
TILNEY:	What play?
SHAKESPEARE:	The play I will write for the King, that will put us in high favour. Witches, the true King of Scotland, vaulting ambition, I can see it all now and it will greatly please James and save your skin. And the King's Men will be saved from jumping into custards and riding fish on rivers, and he will see I can write worthy plays, instead of mere trifles.
TILNEY:	Ah custard again!
SHAKESPEARE:	Very good Sir Edmund.
TILNEY:	Why do you wish to save my skin? We are hardly friends? You are the playwright of the King's Men and I dare say you will still receive commissions to play at Court no matter who is Master of the Revels.
SHAKESPEARE:	You have your faults Sir Edmund, but if I can help you keep your position and further my own, then I am willing to do so.
TILNEY:	But how can we do so?
SHAKESPEARE:	"Seek to know no more. In time you shall know all".

BLACKOUT

LIGHTS UP

Again in the Revels Office.

TILNEY is working at his desk, there is a knock at the door.

TILNEY: Enter.

[*the knocking continues*]

Of course. So much debt from litigation, I can scarce afford a servant now, apart from those Mollies sent by the King.

[TILNEY *walks to the door and opens it. Standing outside is LAURENCE FLETCHER Scottish "in your face" and annoying like a 17th century Wee Jimmy Krankie*]

TILNEY: Yes?

FLETCHER: Sir Edmund Tilney?

TILNEY: Yes.

FLETCHER: The Master of the Revels?

TILNEY: Unless you know of another Knight of the Realm called Tilney?

FLETCHER: Sir Charles, your brother I think? Not a bad laddie, tried to get Mary Queen of Scots on the throne. Didnae go well though, did it?

[*he mimes an execution*]

TILNEY: Get to the point, commencing with who in Hades are you?

FLETCHER: Laurence Fletcher – the English Comedian.

TILNEY: But you're Scottish.

FLETCHER: That's what I do you see? I mix it up a bit, I play with you.

TILNEY: I am a very busy man, what do you want?

FLETCHER: I am the new Sharer in the King's Men.

TILNEY:	Really? And on whose authority?
	[FLETCHER *hands over a letter with a seal*]
FLETCHER:	Jacobus Rex.
TILNEY:	I beg your pardon? The King?
FLETCHER:	Well in a manner of speaking, that's what it says on the seal, it's actually from the Lord Chamberlain.
TILNEY:	Oh what a surprise!
FLETCHER:	Anyway, what was your name again Pal?
TILNEY:	As I said before, Sir Edmund Tilney.
FLETCHER:	Oh aye that's right, I wasnae really listening you ken? Well, hope to see you around Ed.
	[TILNEY *is apoplectic*]
	All my friends call me Fletch.
TILNEY:	Do they really – Fletcher?
	[*enter* SHAKESPEARE. *He has the manuscript of "Macbeth" under his arm and looks confused*]
SHAKESPEARE:	Good day Sir Edmund, I cannot help but notice that your outer chamber is now populated by young men wearing dresses from the Revels wardrobe ...
TILNEY:	Yes Master Shakespeare, His Majesty has seen fit to offer me the er ... assistance of some of his favourite courtiers.
SHAKESPEARE:	How very generous of His Majesty, they look to be very flamboyant young men.
TILNEY:	His Majesty I fear still labours under a misapprehension about me ...
FLETCHER:	You don't want to be ashamed about being a jobby jabber, Ed, you're amongst pals now, and we're not in the Dark Ages, the Tudors have long gone.
SHAKESPEARE:	But the ballad remains the same.

[FLETCHER *suddenly turns on* SHAKESPEARE *and we see a more dangerous side to him*]

FLETCHER: Sorry Pal I didnae quite catch that?

SHAKESPEARE: Nothing. I was just thinking aloud.

FLETCHER: You want to watch that, and you are?

SHAKESPEARE: I am no one, just a writer.

FLETCHER: Is that so? And what do you write? Nothing treasonous, I hope! Not like that Ben Jonson.

SHAKESPEARE: No. I am William Shakespeare of The King's Men.

FLETCHER: I've heard of you! You're the Man! I cannae wait to work with you.

SHAKESPEARE: Really? And pray tell, who are you?

FLETCHER: I am your new Sharer.

SHAKESPEARE: That is news to me.

FLETCHER: Oh I love bringing good news me! I love your work, is this one of yours?

[FLETCHER *goes to shelves and grabs a manuscript*]

"Richard the Third" – on no, cannae be, there's no writer's name on it …

[FLETCHER *throws the manuscript on* TILNEY's *desk,* SHAKESPEARE *looks ill at ease*]

SHAKESPEARE: An oversight I am sure.

[TILNEY *looks at* SHAKESPEARE *and then down at the manuscript.* FLETCHER *goes back to the shelf*]

FLETCHER: This is one of yours, isn't it? "Taming of A Shrew".

SHAKESPEARE: "The" Shrew.

FLETCHER: Same difference, I thought it was shite. You know what you should have done?

SHAKESPEARE:	Do tell.
FLETCHER:	You know Petruchio's servant?
SHAKESPEARE:	Grumio? Yes I do know him, I wrote him.
FLETCHER:	He was shite. You should have made him Scottish. I do a lot of observational stuff in my other job.
SHAKESPEARE:	Oh do you now?
FLETCHER:	I do a lot of character stuff as well, I am trying out some new material, I got a new character, he's called "Sawney", you could make him the servant, give him the lead part, you could call it ...
SHAKESPEARE:	"Sawney the Scot"?
FLETCHER:	That's the one Will! Love it!
SHAKESPEARE:	Happy to have been of service. Now I have some business to attend to with Sir Edmund.
FLETCHER:	You go ahead Lads, I dinnae mind waiting, I'll have a read of old Crookback Richard the Third.
	[FLETCHER *goes to pick up the Richard III script but* TILNEY *places his hand on it*]
SHAKESPEARE:	No. They have need of you at the Globe. I am sure Will Kemp eagerly awaits the arrival of the new comedian. I am sure you will get on like a playhouse on fire.
FLETCHER:	I'd best be going then, refresh my memory, the Globe is???
	[*he points vaguely*]
SHAKESPEARE:	I can give you a short cut that only we theatre folk know. The quickest way is down Deadman's Lane, ignore the stories about the footpads, they welcome the players with open arms.
FLETCHER:	Maybe I'll do a turn for them.

SHAKESPEARE:	Indeed you will.
FLETCHER:	I'll see you later for a bevy Will.
SHAKESPEARE:	[*aside*] If you live that long.
	[FLETCHER *exits*]
SHAKESPEARE:	Who the hell was that?
TILNEY:	That Master Shakespeare, is Laurence Fletcher, the English Comedian.
SHAKESPEARE:	But he's Scottish.
TILNEY:	Yes, we have established that.
SHAKESPEARE:	And he is about as funny as the pox.
TILNEY:	Yes, we have established that also.
SHAKESPEARE:	So why is he being sent to work for the King's Men?
	[TILNEY *throws* FLETCHER's *letter with the seal across to* SHAKESPEARE]
TILNEY:	I don't know, why not ask the King?
	[SHAKESPEARE *reads the letter*]
SHAKESPEARE:	Why is the King sending this idiot here?
TILNEY:	Because Master Shakespeare, he is a better player than we give him credit for.
SHAKESPEARE:	A spy? So his act was nothing more than a clever tale told by a cunning idiot?
TILNEY:	Master Shakespeare you would do well to heed this so called "Idiot". I believe Fletcher is a dangerous man, the King now has his spies everywhere, including here.
	[TILNEY *points to the outer chamber*]
	There are many spying for the girl-King and one is on his way to your playhouse, so the players had better learn to keep their clack boxes shut for a change.
SHAKESPEARE:	Change! We all expected change, but alas there

	is none, the people looked forward to the day "King Jamie got his crown on" – they even made a ballad about it, but the song remains the same.
TILNEY:	I must confess I cannot deal with him, no one is safe, not even you Master Shakespeare.
SHAKESPEARE:	But I am a King's Man.
TILNEY:	Well, maybe he will take you to the Royal Menagerie where he likes to see the Lion and Tiger fight over the dogs, cats and even horses he has thrown to them, maybe he will throw you to them. That is entertainment under King Jamie!
SHAKESPEARE:	All is not lost. I, or should I say we, have a play here that will gain us favour with His Majesty.
	[SHAKESPEARE *hands* TILNEY *the manuscript of "Macbeth"*]
TILNEY:	"The tragedy of Macbeth". "When shall we three met again, in thunder, lightning or in rain ..."
SHAKESPEARE:	I would go no further if I were you Sir Edmund.
TILNEY:	Where did you get this rhyme from?
SHAKESPEARE:	The King's own book. "Demonology".
TILNEY:	Then these are real witches' spells, is that wise?
SHAKESPEARE:	Wise enough to please a King.
	[TILNEY *continues to look through the script*]
TILNEY:	Is it also wise to make a mockery of the King's drinking?
SHAKESPEARE:	What?
TILNEY:	Here "Enter a show of Kings, the latter with a glass in his hand".
SHAKESPEARE:	No Sir Edmund, it is a looking glass.
	[TILNEY *still looks confused*]

SHAKESPEARE:	Allow me to elucidate, Sir Edmund you shall be the King, no treason meant, so where will His Majesty sit?
TILNEY:	In the front of course.
SHAKESPEARE:	Of course, if I may?
	[*he takes up a looking glass and acts this next section out*]
SHAKESPEARE:	Six Kings walk across the stage and divide as they approach His Majesty, the last actor will hold a looking glass in his hand, reflecting the King in the front row, the true heir of Banquo, our rightful King.
TILNEY:	You have learnt well Master Shakespeare.
SHAKESPEARE:	I learnt from you Sir Edmund.
	[TILNEY *continues to flick through the script*]
TILNEY:	Let us get it entered.
	[TILNEY *opens the ledger on his desk and enters the play's details*]
SHAKESPEARE:	I will take my leave of you.
TILNEY:	Master Shakespeare – there's just one more thing.
	[TILNEY *picks up the Richard III script*]
	Of all the plays for our new friend Fletcher to have found, he lights upon "Richard the Third". It only seems like yesterday, that I had to persuade you to write the true history of the Crookbacked King for our late Queen.
SHAKESPEARE:	That is an old play, not fit for a new King.
TILNEY:	I quite agree Master Shakespeare. One thing is troubling me though.
SHAKESPEARE:	May I ask what that is Sir Edmund?
TILNEY:	Why does your name not appear upon this play Master Shakespeare?

SHAKESPEARE:	An oversight.
TILNEY:	Ah an oversight. But you did not forget to sign all of your other plays.
SHAKESPEARE:	I was writing under a great deal of pressure.
TILNEY:	Well you are under pressure now, and it is my right to press you for the truth.
SHAKESPEARE:	But I have just given you the truth.
TILNEY:	No. You have just given me the lie! You did not write this did you? DID YOU!?
	[*a long pause*]
	Your silence says it all. So, if you did not write this play, then who did?
SHAKESPEARE:	You did!
TILNEY:	What?
SHAKESPEARE:	And the Queen did and Sir Thomas More did and Topcliffe did and actually, yes I did too, but last but by no means least, my late departed friend, Kit did.
TILNEY:	Marlowe! I should have known!
SHAKESPEARE:	"Dead Shepherd now I found thy saw of might who ever loved that loved not at first sight". As You Like It".
TILNEY:	I do not like it at all. You have duped me Master Shakespeare.
SHAKESPEARE:	I did not dupe you Sir Edmund I gave you what you asked for.
TILNEY:	So why then did you not write it ALL yourself?
LIGHTS FADE	

Flashback to 1593.

LIGHTS UP on a Stratford upon Avon tavern during the reign of Elizabeth; an old lady MARION HACKETT is seated at a table. SHAKESPEARE enters, an inkhorn around his neck and carries his draft of Richard III under his arm; the HOST greets him.

HOST: Good day to you Sir, your pleasure?

SHAKESPEARE: A tankard of your finest Stratford ale.

HOST: Of course Sir, are you local? I haven't seen you here before.

SHAKESPEARE: Well originally.

HOST: I thought I recognised the accent. I couldn't help noticing Sir, the inkhorn about your neck, are you a lawyer, Sir?

SHAKESPEARE: Some are convinced I am, but no.

HOST: But you write Sir?

SHAKESPEARE: Yes. On occasion.

HOST: May I be so bold as to ask a favour of you Sir?

SHAKESPEARE: Of course.

HOST: Would you write something for me Sir? Nothing very much, just a couple of lines.

SHAKESPEARE: I'd be glad to.

                   [*he dips the quill into the inkhorn*]

HOST: Could you write "Do not ask for credit as a refusal often offends".

SHAKESPEARE: What?

HOST: For behind the counter sir, some people think I am made of money, they would chalk up seven or eight tankards on the slate, then they go outside to "tend the horses", and then they're away.

~99~

SHAKESPEARE:	There you are.
	[SHAKESPEARE *hands a piece of parchment to the* HOST]
	"Neither a borrower or a lender be" and I've signed it.
HOST:	Well I suppose they will understand it, what's your name?
SHAKESPEARE:	William Shakespeare. Who makes a ballad for an alehouse door, shall live in future times for evermore.
	[*the* HOST *exits puzzling over the note.*
	MARION HACKETT *looks up from her beer*]
MARION:	Will? Will Shakespeare?
SHAKESPEARE:	Yes.
MARION:	John's boy! I knew you before you were in breeches.
SHAKESPEARE:	Forgive me, I have been away for some time.
MARION HACKETT:	You put me in one of your plays I heard, you naughty boy. "Marion Hackett the fat alewife of Wincot".
SHAKESPEARE:	Once again forgive me.
MARION:	Come and join me, don't drink on your own. I could do with some company now since I lost my husband.
SHAKESPEARE:	So you no longer keep your alehouse?
MARION:	I haven't for many years Will. Where have you been?
SHAKESPEARE:	London actually.
MARION:	I am pulling your breeches Will. We've all heard about you, writing your fancy plays, even writ one for the Queen I heard.
SHAKESPEARE:	I didn't have much choice, she commanded a play from me.

MARION:	Did she indeed? And did you put me in that one and all?
SHAKESPEARE:	Forgive me for using your name. I recall my father spoke of you and your late husband with much affection.
MARION:	That's nice. Remember me to your father when you see him. How is the family Will? Anne well?
SHAKESPEARE:	She has been nagging me ever since I got up from London.
MARION:	Well, she's right! It can't be easy for her, you down in London most of the time.
SHAKESPEARE:	Don't you start Marion. I am already being nagged at home, and don't get me started on the Master of the Revels.
MARION:	Edmund Tilney? That lovesick moon calf!
SHAKESPEARE:	What! You know Sir Edmund?
MARION:	Oh "Sir" now is he? We did all laugh, when he got jilted by the Mermaid.
SHAKESPEARE:	Mermaid? How many tankards have you had?
MARION:	No listen Will, you were just a boy. You wouldn't remember. We all went over to Kenilworth when the Queen visited Robert Dudley, Earl of Leicester as was, to try to see her. That Edmund organised a masque with mermaids, and he had his eye on the most beautiful one, but she ran off with a Player!
SHAKESPEARE:	And that was Tilney?
MARION:	Course it was, but enough of him, is that your new play?
	[she goes to pick it up]
SHAKESPEARE:	It is, but it's not finished, and don't you spill your beer on that Marion Hackett! It's for the Queen.

MARION:	Is it? Read it to me, like I am Gloriana herself in her Palace! What's it called?
SHAKESPEARE:	"The Tragedy of King Richard the Third – his treacherous plots against his Brother Clarence, the pitiful murder of his innocent nephews – his tyrannical usurping of the throne, his detested life and most deserved death".
MARION:	Oh Will! Those are very harsh words against King Richard. My old granddad used to call him the King of the North, he said Richard was a good King. He reduced taxes, not like some I could mention, and you don't want to start digging up that "Princes in the Tower" thing again.
SHAKESPEARE:	Why?
MARION:	Granddad used to say he reckoned it was old Misery Guts that did for those young boys so he could keep the throne.
SHAKESPEARE:	Misery guts?
MARION:	Lizzie's Grandad.
SHAKESPEARE:	King Henry the Seventh??
MARION:	"King Henry!" I heard many had better claim to the throne than he did. And then them two silly little imposter boys, letting themselves get used, pretending to be the dead Princes, at least one only got put into the kitchen for his stupidity, the other silly sod did the Tyburn jig.
SHAKESPEARE:	[checking in his script] But James Tyrell confessed to the murders, I have it here.
MARION:	Under torture, if you put me on the rack I would say I was the Queen of Sheba.
HOST:	That's enough of that talk now, you have had too much ale, Marion. Master Shakespeare can I have a word?

[HOST *brings* SHAKESPEARE *to one side*]

There are some men in the back parlour, not from round here, from London if you ask me. They've been listening to every word you said, I would be careful if I were you.

SHAKESPEARE: Thank you. I bid you good night. Take care Marion.

MARION: Good night Will. I am sorry, did I say something wrong?

SHAKESPEARE: No Mistress Hackett. You said nothing wrong, far from it.

SHAKESPEARE *exits*

Lights fade to BLACKOUT.

In BLACKOUT we hear voices.

INSTRUMENT: You need a history lesson you old hag!

MARION HACKETT *screams.*

LIGHTS UP

In the Revels Office

TILNEY: Do you mean to say you would change the play
                     you were commanded to write for your Queen
                     on the word of a drunken alewife in a
                     godforsaken tavern?

SHAKESPEARE: I simply listened Sir Edmund, I took your advice,
                     I read Thomas More.

                     [*he produces a book*]

                     Which I now return to you, somewhat late.

TILNEY: Ten years to be precise. But you found it
                     useful?

SHAKESPEARE: In a way.

TILNEY: In what way?

SHAKESPEARE: Terrible history, great food for thought.

TILNEY: I don't follow?

SHAKESPEARE: Although I do not agree with all he did, I cannot
                     deny More was a man of principle. He could
                     have accepted Henry as head of the church,
                     been out of the Tower and home in Chelsea in
                     time for dinner, but he did not. More could not
                     go against what he believed, so what
                     happened? He would not sign the act of
                     Supremacy, so Thomas Cromwell took his
                     books, it's funny how they always go for the
                     books don't they? So yes, I read More, you
                     know he made up much of what he claimed
                     were Richard's speeches don't you? He would
                     have made a good playwright, and I read much
                     more than More.

TILNEY: Like what?

SHAKESPEARE: The last play by Kit Marlow, "The True Tragedy of Richard Duke of Gloucester".

[TILNEY *rushes to his ledgers*]

SHAKESPEARE: It was never completed, therefore you will not find it registered.

TILNEY: You lied to me Master Shakespeare, you lied to the Queen, you were commissioned to write a play showing the detested life of the Crookback King.

SHAKESPEARE: Yes, and how her whole family were so much better and saved the realm from him, let us be as merry as the day is long!

TILNEY: Treason!

SHAKESPEARE: Treason! Is that your answer to everything? When I went to visit my family and I was followed by thugs, when a good old woman who I have known since I was a boy was beaten nigh to death because she dared to suggest that the man who taxed them half to starvation, seized the crown over those who had a better claim to it. But don't you understand? The Tudors are gone, their swansong – a sad old woman with a red wig, white lead upon her face and black teeth.

TILNEY: Who was patron to you and your players, who spoke for you? Yet you never even marked her passing.

SHAKESPEARE: The Queen did much for the players, but, what of the sailors who fought for her bravely against the Armada, what reward did they receive? Many died, broken in mind and body begging on the streets of England, which they fought to save. It is not just the badge of King James I wear upon my sleeve, if truth be told, I wear my heart upon it too. For my dead friend, Marlowe. We drank together, we laughed together, we acted together – badly in my case – and we wrote together, that waterfly Fletcher, wanted me to rewrite "Taming of the Shrew" for him, never, not in my lifetime. You see, Kit and I messed about with an old play about a Shrew, I thought when we had finished with it, we made something of it, does a woman owe duty to her husband? Who is the real Shrew, Kate or Bianca? What is a true marriage? I doubt Petruchio and Kate would have found much to interest them in your "flower of marriage"!

TILNEY: Such jealousy of my work, truly the spite of authors is terrible.

SHAKESPEARE: I did what you asked – I wrote "The Crookback King", and like the Weird Sisters spell, I added a morsel of More, a pinch of Polydore Vergil, I gave him a hump, made him wade in blood, added a gallery of ghosts, and despite him being one of the finest swordsmen in Europe let him be defeated by an unknown Welshman called Henry Tudor – but it needed more …

TILNEY: I think you have plundered enough of Sir Thomas …

SHAKESPEARE: No. If you remember, I said I believed the Queen still deserved better than just a villainous hunchback, a devil from the old morality play, so I remembered Marlowe.

[SHAKESPEARE *picks up the manuscript and turns over till he gets to the speech*]

This part "Clarence's Dream" – the diamonds in the skull's eyes, I don't think I could have written like this at the time, but Kit Marlowe could.

TILNEY: But Marlowe was dead when you wrote this, killed in a tavern brawl.

SHAKESPEARE: He left writing behind him which I saved, and it wasn't a "tavern brawl", it was a respectable woman's house, the truth should be told, but of course history is written by the victors. We will never know truly what happened that fateful day or who else was there with Kit. I came back from Stratford fully intending to walk away from this, I would have offered the Queen, "Love's Labour's Won", but when I got to my lodgings, I find Mistress Montjoy in fear of her life, my scripts destroyed by a so-called "instrument" of Richard Topcliffe, I realised then, this play was clearly important and I was not prepared to put my friends and families lives at risk, so I gave you the play, but I vowed it would be on my terms.

TILNEY: Terms? You dare to dictate terms to the Master of the Revels?

SHAKESPEARE: I didn't need to, I was waylaid by Thomas Kyd, I offered to help him move his few possessions from the garret he shared with Marlow, Kyd was not an easy man I admit, but why crush his hands so he could not write again?

TILNEY: That was Topcliffe, I had nothing to do with that.

SHAKESPEARE: Kyd stood up to Topcliffe's thug, and it allowed me to bundle up what Marlowe had written of **his** Richard the Third and add it to my heady mix.

[TILNEY *starts to scrabble through the manuscript manically*]

TILNEY: Where? Which is which? Which is your hand and which is Marlowe's?

SHAKESPEARE: I cannot remember, it was many years ago.

TILNEY: But this must be properly entered into my ledgers …

SHAKESPEARE:	Best forget it Sir Edmund, it was of its time, like the "Isle of Dogs".
TILNEY:	You did know of that abomination! Why did you lie to me?
SHAKESPEARE:	What are lies, but stories told well?
TILNEY:	This was no innocent tale Shakespeare. Did you read it all?
SHAKESPEARE:	I recall they wrote stuff like, "the Isle of Dogs has burrs and thorns that trip you up and hold you back, called lawyers and lords" made fun of Churchmen, and some bad jokes about the Russians, fear not I wager they will be our friends for all times, so forget the Isle of Dogs let it sink into a sea of oblivion. Sir Edmund, everyone did well from the Crookback, the Queen got her play, you got the praise for the delivery of the piece, Burbage got his greatest role. Did I ever tell you of the court lady who wanted Burbage to come to her as Richard, but I got there first, and …
TILNEY:	You said "William the Conqueror came before Richard the Third".
SHAKESPEARE:	You know that story?
TILNEY:	All London knows that story! I cannot trust you, you have betrayed myself and the Queen.
SHAKESPEARE:	Very well, if it makes you any happier I shall go to the Queen's tomb and beg forgiveness.
TILNEY:	Yes, make mock, all I see is betrayal, you can never trust a player, whether he be in rags or passing himself off as a gentleman and you may be a King's Man, but you are not a gentleman.
SHAKESPEARE:	Maybe if your mermaid at Kenilworth had not abandoned you for a player you would not hate them so.

TILNEY:	Who told you that, who told you of Kenilworth?
SHAKESPEARE:	The same lady who told me of her thoughts on Richard the Third and Henry the Seventh. That good alewife, Marion Hackett.
TILNEY:	She should know her place.
SHAKESPEARE:	Oft times the common people do talk common sense ...
TILNEY:	Do they indeed? I have never noticed it.
SHAKESPEARE:	Perhaps if you met them once or twice you might notice it, perhaps if you actually visited the playhouses, and see how they enjoy the plays you graciously permit to be performed ...
TILNEY:	You hypocrite! Man of the people are you Shakespeare? Then how many of your beloved common people, will be able to attend your new indoor playhouse? How many stinkards will be there? None! As well you know!
SHAKESPEARE:	The decision to go to Blackfriars, was Burbage's, not mine, what could I do? He is the leading actor, and Chief Sharer, and as you told me yourself, I am just a common player and sometime writer. But we will still perform for the groundlings at the Globe as they have been the very making of me.
TILNEY:	They say a man is known by the company he keeps.
SHAKESPEARE:	Why can you not afford to be gracious Sir Edmund? When you winked and smiled at me I thought you the finest gallant I had seen.
TILNEY:	What are you talking about?
SHAKESPEARE:	Kenilworth Castle. We all came over from Stratford to catch a sight of the "Princely Pleasures" for the Queen, and for a young boy on his father's shoulders trying to see the Revel that you were in charge of, I was in awe of you,

for you seemed to have the most magical task in the world, and you spoke to Mermaids.

TILNEY: I did, but she was no Mermaid, she was the Lady of the Lake.

LIGHTS FADE

LIGHTS UP

The background suggests Kenilworth Castle. Princely Pleasures 1575 The young TILNEY is addressing an offstage team.

TILNEY: Is all prepared with the dragon? Where are the children of the Chapel Royal? This is no time for them to be playing conkers! Tell them they are needed at West gate for the cave of the Sybil, now where is the Lady of the Lake and her nymphs?

[*the* LADY OF THE LAKE *appears wearing diaphanous garments she is very alluring!*]

And who else could you be than that Goddess, the Lady of the Lake herself?

[LADY OF THE LAKE *spits out water over him, and she fishes into her cleavage for a hankerchief and blows her nose noisily*]

LADY OF THE LAKE: So my gracious gallant, are you in charge?

TILNEY: Well in a manner of speaking, all is under the command of the Master of the Revels.

LADY OF THE LAKE: Clearly by your finery that is you then?

TILNEY: Well not yet ...

LADY OF THE LAKE: Not yet? I do not follow Sir.

TILNEY: The Master is Sir Thomas Blagrave over yonder, but I am sure I will be the next one.

LADY OF THE LAKE: Oh right, and Master of the Revels is a good job is it?

TILNEY: There is much to recommend it, I attend with Sir Thomas at all the Queen's Palaces, to be honest it is really me that arranges Revels, we receive fine wine, fine food, the same as is served at the Queen's table.

LADY OF THE LAKE: Well Sir I clearly see you are the [*loaded with innuendo*] "coming man".

TILNEY: I certainly hope to be.

LADY OF THE LAKE: Now clearly you are the man I need to speak with. I am not being funny or nothing, but am I going to be in that lake for long? It's just I have a delicate constitution and if I get an ague it will go straight to my chest.

[*flirting with the young* TILNEY *she sticks her chest out*]

TILNEY: Would it indeed? Well I must say to you ...

[*the other actor comes in as a bumbling menial with thick glasses and clutching a parchment*]

MENIAL: I've lost the sausage man!

TILNEY: How dare you! I am Edmund Tilney, assistant to the Master of the Revels, do I look like I am in charge of itinerant food vendors?

MENIAL: Well you had better sort it out, the Queen is on her way.

TILNEY: Why the hell would the Queen meet a sausage man?

LADY OF THE LAKE: Well good sir, maybe even a Queen likes a bit of meat!

[*she giggles coarsely to the unseen nymphs*]

TILNEY: Ladies please! Let me see that.

[TILNEY *takes the parchment and screws up his eyes to read it*]

That says "savage man" not "sausage man", look there he is polishing his club.

LADY OF THE LAKE: [*giggles*] I could do that for him or for anyone else in need Young Sir!

TILNEY: [*shouting into audience to unseen performer*] Gird up your lionskin and take your club and hide in that holly bush ready to reveal yourself to the Queen.

LADY OF THE LAKE: Let's hope he doesn't catch his lion skin on a holly leaf or he will reveal more of himself to the Queen than she expected! Eh girls? [*more coarse giggles*] What was your name again?

TILNEY: Edmund Tilney.

LADY OF THE LAKE: [*pointing off*] Well Edmund, my fellow nymphs think you may have found your sausage man if that fellow's codpiece is anything to go by, eh girls? Who is he?

TILNEY: A common player by the name of [*he checks the list*] Gabriel Spenser, he is to be the Latin Poet.

[TILNEY *shouts offstage*]

TILNEY: Master Spencer, is that a flask of wine I see in your hand? You had best con your part rather than carouse.

LADY OF THE LAKE: Ooh bit harsh! One might even suppose you to be jealous of him.

TILNEY: Jealous of a common player?

LADY OF THE LAKE: He does have a lovely voice.

TILNEY: Yes, he may speak well, sing and swordfight, but I have something over him.

LADY OF THE LAKE: And what is that?

TILNEY: Power! I can command him and dismiss him at my will, and I can advance you too. Before you go my Lady of the Lake, may I know your name?

LADY OF THE LAKE: Jane Nightwork.

MENIAL: Appropriate if you ask me.

TILNEY: Lady Jane, when our revel is over tonight, I shall be waiting here by yonder Hawthorn break.

LADY OF THE LAKE: I shall bear that in mind, Good Master of the Revels, to be!

[she exits]

MENIAL: Master Tilney, I fear there is a problem with King Arthur's Knights, Sir Galahad likes not his costume and has just pushed Sir Lancelot in the horse trough.

TILNEY: Players!

LIGHTS DOWN

LIGHTS UP

Back in the Revels Office.

SHAKESPEARE: So, what happened may I ask?

               [TILNEY *is silent*]

               She did not come, did she Sir Edmund?

TILNEY: No Shakespeare. Since you ask, she went with a player.

SHAKESPEARE: Forgive me Sir Edmund, from what you have described she seems marvellous forward, it may be that she was …

TILNEY: She was a Bankside whore! Yes of course she was, but for a young man making his way in Court do you think I realised that? She made a fool of me, she and that filthy player, Gabriel Spencer.

               [TILNEY's *rage is frightening as he rants and sweeps plays off shelves*]

               Plays, filthy plays, are the inventions of the Devil. Players, writers, are nothing, do you hear me? Nothing! Just masters of vice, teachers of wantoness, spurs to impurity, I loathe them as long as I will live!

               [*he ends up on the floor surrounded by plays.* SHAKESPEARE *pauses then goes to him and helps him up*]

SHAKESPEARE: I am sorry Sir Edmund, let me help you with these.

               [*he indicates the strewn scripts*]

TILNEY: Leave them Master Shakespeare, it will give the King's young men something to do. Leave it for my successor, oh yes Sir George Buck is already named, you will get on well with him, he thinks the Crookback was no villain.

SHAKESPEARE: Does he indeed?

[SHAKESPEARE *reaches into his bag and produces a parchment which he hands over and* TILNEY *tries to decipher* SHAKESPEARE's *writing*]

TILNEY: [*reading with difficulty*] "The King of the North?" What is this?

SHAKESPEARE: It is but notes, ideas nothing more, oft times pictures come into my head, and I saw one such, of the King, the crown lying uneasily upon his head, pacing the palace, ever fearful of the Princes coming back alive ...

TILNEY: An excellent image Master Shakespeare, why did you not put it in your play for the Queen?

SHAKESPEARE: [*taking back the manuscript*] Because the King who paces the Palace, fearful of the princes' return, is not Richard the Third, but Henry the Seventh, I could not show this, I fear it would have caused offence.

TILNEY: Offence! Master Shakespeare short of you shitting in the Queen's carriage then using her favourite lapdog to wipe your arse with, I can think of no better way to cause offence to the late Queen than to suggest that her grandfather wished the death of the princes!

SHAKESPEARE: [*picking up the notes*] I would like to have had one more attempt at Richard, but this is not for now, but for some future time. Let them decide if he is "The King of the North" as I started him in Harry Sixth, or the "bottled spider" I ended him as in Richard the Third. They may have a choice, I for my family's sake did not. This is for a time when princes may even work for a living, maybe in Raleigh's colonies in the New World, or even stand trial for misdemeanours.

TILNEY: I would be careful of mentioning Raleigh in the King's hearing, he is out of favour, and we must stay in favour, which I am sure we will be with "Mac ..."

SHAKESPEARE: Shh! I have a conceit Sir Edmund, His Majesty is superstitious, so, what say you we "noise about" that the actors must not speak the name of the play, it being cursed, but rather flatter the King by calling it "The Scottish Play".

TILNEY: An excellent idea – Shall see you on Thursday?

SHAKESPEARE: [*surprised*] You will attend rehearsal?

TILNEY: I shall, and thank you ... Will.

SHAKESPEARE: You are most welcome. May I call you "Edmund"?

[*a long pause*]

TILNEY: No.

SHAKESPEARE: Of course not. You will never see me as a gentleman.

[*he picks up his bag, goes to leave, then turns back*]

You mentioned Spencer was the player at Kenilworth who stole your first love, he was killed by Ben Jonson was he not?

TILNEY: Was he indeed?

SHAKESPEARE: Yes, Ben loves to relate the tale of how he fought Spencer despite his weapon being 10 inches longer, I assumed he meant his sword, but you know Ben's idea of humour! You often had Ben released from prison, and clearly you had little love for Spencer. So, did Ben, on your orders? [SHAKESPEARE *mimes throat cutting*]

TILNEY:	Master Shakespeare, to quote your excellent "Scottish Play", "seek to know no more".
SHAKESPEARE:	Good day then Sir Edmund.
	[SHAKESPEARE *exits.*
	TILNEY *starts to pick up the scattered playscripts, he looks at one*]
TILNEY:	"The Tragedy of King Richard the Third containing his treacherous plots against his Brother Clarence, the pitiful murder of his innocent nephews, his tyrannical usurpation – his most detested life and most deserved death", well you know what you are getting there, just one thing is missing.
	[TILNEY *picks up a quill and adds to the front page*]
	"By William Shakespeare … Gent."
	[*he replaces it on the shelf*]

SLOW FADE TO BLACKOUT

THE END

Author Biographies

Clive Greenwood began as a actor at the age of 14. He started writing comedy sketches with "Newsrevue" then with his own sketch show "Out of Order" which transferred to radio and led to him writing for children's TV show "Wysiwyg". His first stage play "Goodbye; the (after)life of Cook & Moore" enjoyed sell out runs in Edinburgh and London, and he has just completed "Laurel & Hancock" for production in 2022. He has written scripts for many historic sites, including Greenwich Painted Hall, Kenilworth Castle, The National Archives, Hampton Court, and the V&A, and has just joined the writing team for Rory Bremner's new show, and written a new radio pilot "Trapped on the telly".

Jason Wing is an actor and writer from West London. He joined the Glynn Knowles Drama Group at a young age and was encouraged to write Plays for the Group to perform. His first play "The Christmas Mystery" was performed by the Group at the Battersea Arts Festival and he won an award from the Mayor of Streatham. Jason went on to study at the Drama Centre via a Sir Anthony Hopkins scholarship and has been working in theatre, television and film as both an actor and writer since he graduated. His career was launched by the director Jonathan Miller in a production of "The Beggar's Opera" at Wiltons Music Hall.

www.ingramcontent.com/pod-product-compliance
Lightning Source LLC
Chambersburg PA
CBHW021222260626
47172CB00002B/562